D1528931

Somebody's Secrets

Talkeetna, Volume 2

L.J. Breedlove

Published by L.J. Breedlove, 2020.

SOMEBODY'S SECRETS

First edition. September 19, 2020.

Written by L.J. Breedlove.

Editor's Note

Sitka is a beautiful city, as the characters say repeatedly throughout this book. I was privileged to live there years ago. Although the setting is real, this book is a work of fiction. Its events are drawn from a number of towns across the state — as well as throughout the country — that are confronting issues of racism and policing. Alaska has unique problems given the isolation of many of its communities, but the role of police in the community needs to be examined by us all.

For some communities, the issues go beyond a few bad apples. When the corruption and racism starts at the top, it will contaminate the whole department, and harm the entire community.

The Sitka in this book doesn't exist. For instance, although during my time there was a 3 1/2 Mile Club, it's no longer there. The first class Shee Atika restaurant is also gone. Things change. And they will continue to change. But the beauty of Sitka lingers, so it seemed fitting that it's the town Paul Kitka calls home.

This book is dedicated to Black Lives Matter with the hope that it will also improve the relationship between police and Native Americans who statistically fare even worse at the hands of law enforcement in this country.

Prologue

(Sitka, Alaska, present day)

"We've got a problem," Police Chief Duke Campbell said without even so much as a good morning.

Bar owner Ben Daniels stifled a sigh. In the 30 plus years — could that be right? He did the math and winced — in the nearly 40 years he'd known the man, he didn't think they had ever had a conversation that didn't start out, "We've got a problem." All too often, the truth was Campbell had a problem, and now it was going to become his as well.

He forced himself to listen to his phone call.

"So, this girl and that Kitka boy come waltzing into the courthouse and fill out a public records request for all the documents pertaining to death of Kitka's father, and to the deaths in the jail between the years 1975 and 1982."

OK, this was a problem, thought Campbell.

"Back up. Who's the girl?"

"I told you." Campbell was impatient. "Her name's Karin Wallace. She's a biology professor, doing some kind of research with Fish and Game for the season. Apparently, her father may have been one of the men who died."

Not a girl, Daniels thought. She'd have to be in her 30s. And a professor. She wasn't stupid, then, although he'd found that professors were often narrowly focused. And of course, a Kitka would be involved. You didn't need ghosts to be haunted by a dead man — his children did the job just fine.

"Jonas Kitka?" he asked. Please let it be Jonas, not Paul. Jonas could be handled. Paul would be another matter. He thanked God that Paul stayed away from Sitka. Away from the past.

"Yeah, yeah, Jonas Kitka. So I ask the city attorney to tell them no, they can't have the records. Jesus, they're 30 years old. Even Luke's death is nearly 20 years ago. But he says if we have the records, we

1

need to turn them over, because we're talking about possible wrongful deaths."

Ben frowned. "I thought the coroner ruled Luke's death justified in the inquest."

"It was. But we still have files, maybe. Maybe they'll not be findable." He sounded sly, or as if he were trying to be sly. Daniels stifled another sigh.

"Chief, I just don't see this as a big problem." Maybe he was just tired. Or maybe he'd learned patience. Most problems burned themselves out without any need for intervention, he'd learned. He wished he'd learned it earlier. Back in the day, he thought he had to solve the problems or risk everything. Which is why this problem never seemed to go away.

"Yeah, well I do. And furthermore, I think Hank Petras is becoming a problem too."

"Hank?" Hank had become the *defacto* enforcer 20 years ago when he'd shown up on the police force and demonstrated his willingness to do whatever was asked of him.

"Rumor has it, he's got a safety net squirreled away, and he's planning to use it for a cushy retirement." The chief was still belligerent. "After all the money we've funneled his way."

Money he'd earned the hard way, Daniels thought. "Chief he can't out us without outing himself."

"He could if he cut a deal with the other Kitka."

OK, he conceded, Campbell might have a point there. But still. Nothing needed to be done now. He said as much to the Chief.

"I disagree. But I can handle it. If you want to sit at your bar and fantasize about Florida and an old folks home, that's fine. But I'm not ready to go out of here yet, and I most certainly don't plan to leave here in cuffs." He hung up without giving Daniels a chance to reply.

Daniels hung up the phone slowly. This bar, appropriately called The Club, faced the road and was dark and cave-like, but his office in the back of the building had a large plate glass window that looked over the bay. He'd been in Sitka nearly 40 years and he never got tired of the views or the beauty of the water surrounded by tree-covered mountains that sloped steeply down to the shores. Sitka ran along the edge of Baranof Island, stretching from the old pulp mill site to the east of him, into the town proper, and then out to the ferry terminal. It spilled across the bridge to a separate island where Mount Edgecombe's snow-covered peak dominated the views to the west. Beautiful country.

He'd come in here in 1964 as an 18-year-old who'd enlisted in the Coast Guard to avoid the draft, and he'd never left. Mustered out here in '68, used his savings to buy a bar, and started building it. He reinvested his money in real estate, much to the jeers of Chief Campbell, and even of Swede. Swede Johannsen was born and raised in Sitka, and his family had controlled the Sitka Fish Processing Plant — SFPP — since God was a pup. Swede understood the value of owning something, but he didn't have the drive to own a third of the town. He smiled a bit. Well, he probably didn't own quite that much, but he owned a lot. He'd married, raised a family. He'd become a power in Sitka and was in large part responsible for Sitka's growth and success. He was proud, goddamit, and he deserved to be part of what they built.

There had been some hard things, hard choices along the way. He'd always known that the steps they took to protect Sitka during the '70s upheavals and to protect the SFPP from the unions were going to come back to bite them. And if one of them hadn't been the chief of police at the time, they would never have gotten away with it.

Maybe it would have been better if they hadn't. Especially when it meant they'd had to take further action.... He turned away from that thought.

So, was Duke right? Did this require additional action? Did they really have a problem that would prevent his retirement? He was beginning to feel the creakiness in his knees, and he'd like to try his hand at golf on a real course. He had been one of the backers for the Sitka golf course five years ago, but all they could fit in was nine holes, and while the scenery was beautiful, finding an overshot ball could be a real bitch.

He caught his reflection in the window as he turned back to his desk. Pretty good for 67, he thought. His hair was cut short, which de-emphasized the receding hairline and the gray, and emphasized his strong features. He was six-foot, still strong as an ox — had to be to run bars for fishermen, Coasties and loggers — and had managed to avoid much of a gut. He was healthy, still in his prime, and he was damn going to enjoy his retirement. His sons were poised to take over — they would have a good income coming in — and he could come visit his grandchildren during fishing season every year.

Really, he thought, the problem wasn't Jonas Kitka or what's her name, something Wallace. The problem was Duke Campbell. He was hotheaded, impetuous, didn't like to be challenged, and it had only gotten worse as he'd aged. He'd been the police chief for 30-some years, and he had grown arrogant with it. No one had the right to challenge him, and his reactions got more extreme every year.

He thought about that, and then he picked up the phone and dialed a number.

"Swede," he said to the owner of the fish packing sheds. "We've got a problem."

Chapter 1

(Anchorage, Alaska. Present day. Monday.)

Candace Marshall looked around at the friends who had come to the Anchorage airport to cheer her on as she took the final step to a private pilot's license. The morning was chilly, but the sun was out. It was April in Anchorage. She tucked her hands under her armpits and jogged a bit, her braid hitting her between her shoulder blades. Nerves mostly. Everyone stood quietly, sipping Starbucks coffee — a treat they couldn't get in Talkeetna. The three youngest Abbott children played chase around the legs of their parents and the other adults. The oldest one was listening to his father and grandfather talk.

Candace — Dace — smiled, almost in disbelief, at the collection of friends she'd found in the last nine months: a handful of pilots, a family with four kids, and a state patrol lieutenant. More friends than she'd had at any point in her 29 years. She took a deep breath and tried to stand straighter. Moved her shoulders back, stretching out the kinks. She didn't want to let these people down.

Lanky Purdue, a tall, lean, Sitka spruce of a man in his late 60s — Dace was probably one of the few who knew his real age, only because she did payroll and taxes — was talking with his son-in-law Bill Abbott. Lanky was her boss, and he'd been instrumental in most of her flying lessons. He owned Purdue's Flight Service in Talkeetna and specialized in flights around Denali. Since last September she'd been the office manager at the Flight Service. Knowing she was appreciated there had gone a long way to giving her back some confidence in herself.

Well, maybe it was confidence for the first time, she thought. Life hadn't inspired her to have much confidence so far.

Two of Purdue's pilots had flown out as well — carrying the Abbott family. One, Adam Black, was in his mid-30s. He had patiently flown with her as she clocked her flight hours. He hadn't ever raised his voice, and she'd seen his knuckles get white only once when she'd had to land in an unexpected snowstorm. Even then, he'd let her land the plane. Rafe Martinez was as outgoing as Adam was quiet. He was in his early 20s, brash, but he made Dace laugh. He'd coached her through all of the book knowledge she'd had to learn. She hadn't expected there'd be so much, and she got frustrated, especially with maps and laying out her flight plans. He'd tease, and they'd go back at it.

The fourth pilot, Elijah Calhoun, didn't fly anymore. His haunted eyes made her ache; he'd lost his family in a crash a few years back. He'd been the only one to survive. But last fall he'd guided her through her first solo flight — she rolled her eyes as she thought of it — and he'd been her friend ever since. She'd been kidnapped by a murderer. She had knocked her kidnapper out with the fire extinguisher, and then taken over the plane in midair. Elijah Calhoun had been on the ground, riding shotgun in Paul Kitka's red Corvette, talking her through flying the plane. It was then she'd decided to learn to fly.

She looked around for Paul, who smiled when she caught his eye. She blushed a bit, ducking her head. She wasn't sure what to think about Paul Kitka, a lieutenant in the Alaska State Patrol, and her housemate. He'd believed in her when she'd been accused of her husband's murder. She could never thank him enough for that. As for what else there might be between them.... She shied away from finishing that thought. Stop it, she admonished herself. You were a married woman, you're not some blushing virgin with her first crush. It didn't help.

"Ms. Marshall? Are you ready?" The FAA pilot who would administer the test interrupted her thoughts. Candace nodded. She handed her coffee to Mary Abbott. Mary smiled.

"You'll do fine, honey," she said. Mary, once Dace's landlady, was now her best friend. Dace smiled back. Breathe, she reminded herself, and drew in a big breath and let it out. You can do this.

"Why don't you walk me through your safety check then?" The testing pilot, Robert Brown, gestured toward the single-engine Cessna sitting on the tarmac not far from her and her friends.

She took one last look at her boss, who gave her an encouraging nod. Lanky had been a bush pilot before she was born, she reminded herself. If he said she was ready, she was ready. He had trained her, although all of his pilots had been eager to help. Anything to keep her happy, Rafe Martinez had informed her. If she was happy, then she'd stay as Purdue's office manager, and that made everyone's life easier. She was setting a new record as manager, previously held by a drunk who had lasted nine weeks. She had been in Talkeetna for nine months. She shook her head. It seemed longer than that; as if nine months ago, her life had finally gotten started for real.

There was a nip in the air, but it was a sunny day — a nice day for April. Candace shivered a little, more from excitement and anxiety than from the weather. Brown glanced down at her and smiled. "Relax," he said. "This is just a formality. You've been trained by one of the legends in this business. If Lanky Purdue says you're ready for a license, far be it from me to disagree."

A smile twitched at the corner of her mouth at his echo of her own thoughts. She nodded in acknowledgement of his comment. Confidence, she told herself. Have confidence.

They walked around the plane, and Brown asked her questions about the plane, its maintenance and its capabilities, as she checked things over. She was meticulous, even though she and Lanky had just flown the plane in from Talkeetna. As much as anything, she wanted to make Lanky proud. The two got into the cockpit, and Dace ran through the tests and preparations there, following the chart carefully. She had the checklist memorized, but she didn't deviate from the safety of the card. Brown nodded in approval.

"OK, let's take this baby up," he said smiling.

The group on the ground was quiet until the plane taxied down the runway and was off. Purdue sighed. "Well the hardest part is over," he said. He was more nervous than Dace was.

"Well, until she has to land," said Paul Kitka.

Elijah Calhoun snorted. "Not a problem. She landed a plane her first time up. She'll do it again."

Everyone snickered. They'd all been involved last fall when Dace took over the plane midflight. It had made quite the sensational story. Most non-pilots were lucky if they survived a landing like that. Dace had managed a good landing — and she'd subdued her kidnapper as well.

"She's a natural," Purdue said gruffly. He loved his daughter and grandchildren — but as he'd taught her about flying over the winter, he'd come to love Dace as a second daughter. His daughter Mary had never been interested in planes. Dace loved being in the air and loved the machines as much as he did.

Mary squeezed his hand, and he smiled down at her. It was good to see her enjoying being in Anchorage. He had been afraid that would never happen. Her husband, Bill Abbott, held her other hand. Bill was the size of a small 'dozer, but he was gentle with Mary and their kids.

"So, you going to let her take customers up?" Bill Abbott asked. "Who'll keep the office straight then?"

"It's just a private license," Purdue said. "Not commercial." He searched the sky, looking for the return of the plane. He had every confidence in Dace's abilities, but things could always go wrong. He sighed with relief when he saw it heading back.

Paul Kitka was also watching the plane. Lanky Purdue wondered briefly what the relationship was between the two. Now that Candace was no longer a murder suspect, had Paul finally found a woman he could settle down with? Candace was still sharing his house, although she denied they were anything more than friends. Purdue hadn't heard any gossip about Paul and the ladies since she'd moved in. And that didn't even seem possible.

Kitka was just under six-foot, part of the heritage of his white mother, with the warm brown skin and black hair of his Tlingit father. He had a reputation as a ladies' man, but at 36 it was time for him to settle down, Purdue thought. Maybe with Candace, although she might have some trust issues to resolve after her abusive husband. He sighed.

"What's that sigh for?" Mary asked, smiling up at him. He shook his head. Should leave the matchmaking to her anyway, he thought. She probably knew exactly what was going on and had figured out how to bring the two together.

The plane landed smoothly, and everyone sighed with relief. "She did it!" Purdue said as the plane taxied to a stop in front of them. The crowd rushed toward Candace as she crawled out of the cockpit. Robert Brown came around from the other side.

"A perfect flight," he said, shaking Candace's hand. He handed her the results of his observations. "Keep that until you get your pilot's certificate in the mail," he said. "But you're good to go."

Purdue's oldest grandson Andy cheered, and the others clapped. Candace smiled, and then gave Purdue a hug. "Thank you," she said softly.

"My pleasure," he said, hugging her back. Then everyone was hugging her, except for Paul. She glanced around, missing him, and seeing he had stepped away to take a call.

Paul Kitka stood a bit away, with a finger in one ear so he could hear. "Mom?" he said. "What's wrong?" He loved his mother, and they talked regularly on Sunday afternoons. He couldn't remember the last time she'd called him during the week. His jaw clenched. Something had to be wrong. "Are you OK?"

"I'm fine," she said reassuringly. He didn't relax, waiting for the rest of it. "It's Jonas."

Figures, Paul thought. "What's he done now?"

There was a moment of silence, and then his mother whispered, "They've arrested him, Paul. They say he murdered a cop."

Paul's jaw clenched. "He what?"

"He didn't do it, Paul, I know he didn't. I know he's wild, but he wouldn't do that."

"Who, Ma?"

She sighed. "Petras. They say he killed Hank Petras."

Shit, Paul thought. His mom may not have thought Jonas did it, but she'd be the only one. Eighteen years ago, Police Officer Hank Petras killed his father, Luke Kitka, Jr., and was exonerated. No one would have any problems believing that one of Luke's wild sons would have killed him.

"Paul, please. I know you and Jonas don't get along, but I need you. Please. Come to Sitka. There's no way Jonas is going to get a fair trial here, you know that."

Paul sighed. He looked over at Candace still circled by their friends. "I'll come as soon as I can get there," he said.

He closed the phone and joined the group. He put a smile on his face that he didn't feel and gave Dace a big hug. "Congratulations!" he said smiling down at her. "So, are you ready to take on customers?"

Dace laughed, pretty with more color in her checks than usual. "Can't do that," she said, "but I can give you a ride home." Like she'd be able to compete with that Corvette he and Calhoun drove in.

He laughed and hugged her again. "Actually, I was hoping for a ride to Sitka," he admitted. "Lanky?"

Purdue frowned slightly, mentally reviewing the demands of the trip. "Should be OK," he said. "You pay expenses; she flies you for free. Every new pilot needs a maiden voyage."

"OK then!" Dace said, happily. "When do you want to go?"

"Now?" he asked.

Everyone looked at him. "This police business, Paul?" Lanky Purdue asked.

Paul shook his head. "No. Personal. Mom needs me to come home."

Conversation swirled up again, as Mary and Purdue haggled over what would need to be done before Dace could leave. "She doesn't even have a change of clothes with her," Mary exclaimed.

Dace ignored them. She could buy things in Sitka if they stayed long, that didn't worry her. She was more interested in Purdue's thinking out loud about fuel and time. But her focus was on Paul's face. "What's wrong?" she asked quietly.

He shook his head. "Not here," he said. "We'll have time to talk on the way."

The next hour passed quickly. Mary packed a lunch bought from the stands inside the Anchorage airport, and put together a small overnight bag of underwear, jeans and T-shirts, all Candace wore anyway. Dace and Purdue filed a flight plan and worked out the details of her trip. Paul Kitka made phone calls. Candace watched him worriedly.

"This isn't just a fun trip to Sitka," Bill Abbott said quietly watching Paul along with her. "Something's wrong. Too bad. Sitka's a beautiful place."

"You've been there?"

Bill nodded. "On company business." Bill Abbott worked on the North Slope for Arco. "It's green and lush. Lots of trees. The ocean is beautiful. It's an old town, lots of history." He snorted. "Lots of Paul's history."

"You got ideas about what this is about?"

He shook his head. "I've heard a little gossip. Not enough to help I'm afraid. He'll have to tell you."

She nodded. Maybe he would. Maybe not. Neither of them were good at talking about their feelings. They both had secrets they didn't share. Really, they shared a house, and not a lot more than that, although no one believed it. Paul had quite a reputation, she'd found. But he'd never made a move on her. In fact, today was the second time he'd ever touched her — a hug now, and a hug nine months ago when he'd raced his red Corvette across the state to beat her plane when she'd been kidnapped. That had been a promising hug, she'd thought, but then they'd retreated, and she didn't know how to fix that. She'd developed skills in avoiding touch in her marriage, not seeking it out.

It was almost noon when Dace headed the plane back down the runway with Paul sitting in the copilot's seat. She relaxed as the plane hit cruising speed. As noisy as the plane was, it was soothing after all the hubbub of the morning. She let the sounds of the plane sooth her. It was truly a glorious day to be in the air. There was nothing like it. The sun was brighter above the clouds, which were fluffy white today. The sky was a crystal blue. She sighed with pleasure.

Neither of them said anything for the first hour. Paul seemed lost in his own thoughts, and Dace was content to focus on her plane and the simple demands of flying.

"You going to tell me about it?" she asked as they headed more to the south over the southeast islands. Juneau would be coming up shortly. And Sitka wasn't far from that.

"Too hard to shout about it," Paul shouted back. They didn't have headphones. Truth was, he wasn't sure what to say. That his father had been the town drunk? That one morning he was out waving a gun and taking potshots as people commuted to the lumber plant for work and a cop had shot and killed him? Not memories he wanted to shout over the roar of the plane.

Dace opened her mouth to say something, but then just nodded. She refocused on flying and left Paul to his thoughts.

Candace gasped at the beauty below her as she sank below the cloud layer over Sitka. Snow-topped mountains, dark green forests, blue water. She could see why this was a popular port with the tour ships.

She made contact with the airport tower and circled over the bay just looking. When she started studying the airport runway, she swallowed hard. "I thought they landed jets on this runway," she shouted to Kitka.

He nodded. "Alaska Airlines lands here three times a day going each way," he shouted back.

"On that runway?"

He grinned. "Yup. The flight attendants used to have the cherry tomato race in the aisle when they landed — the descent is steep enough the tomatoes would roll all the way down the aisle to the front of the plane."

She shook her head in disbelief. Plenty of runway for her small plane, but she couldn't imagine landing a jet here. Good Alaska pilots are crazy, she reminded herself. Bad ones are dead. What did that make her? She grinned.

"We used to come out here and just watch the planes land and take off," Kitka said. "I've seen the planes crow-hop in the snow. Once, I saw a plane get enough lift by running off the end of the runway. It's built on a dike out into the bay, so he had about 30 feet of lift when his wheels left the ground."

Candace shuddered, but she noticed that Kitka didn't have any problem talking about this over the roar of the plane. Just personal stuff. And who was she to criticize? She couldn't talk about personal things either — not even to save her life. Literally, last fall, Paul had to figure things out for himself, because she couldn't say the words "he abused me." Still couldn't say them out loud. She knew all about words you just couldn't get out.

She smiled with delight when she executed a perfect touchdown and taxied to the tie downs. She shut off the engine, and hopped out to make arrangements for the plane, but Kitka was already dealing with it.

"Come on," he said. "We can catch a taxi into town, get some supper before I call Mom for a ride."

"Your mom got a name?"

He snorted. "Elizabeth Crowe Kitka, professor of English literature."

"And Sitka's got taxis?"

"So to speak." Kitka opened the door into the small airport, and 20 paces later, led her out the other side. A Sitka taxi — it said so on the door — stood idle at the curb. It was a dirty, battered Toyota probably 20 years old. She thought the original color had been blue.

"Not many car-proud people here," Kitka said, interpreting her look accurately. "There's only 30 miles of road. The salt eats cars up something fierce. It costs money to bring a car in here on the ferry, and it costs almost as much to get rid of a junker. No space for junkyards. So, people drive them for as long as they can." He leaned in the window, said something to the driver, and then opened the back door for Candace. He got in the front.

"So where are we now?" Dace asked, looking around with interest.

"This is Mount Edgecombe," Paul answered. "Coast Guard base, airport and Indian Boarding School."

The taxi driver, an Alaskan Native man of 50 or so looked at Paul. "Paul Kitka, aren't you?"

Paul nodded.

"Been awhile since you've been home," the man observed as he crossed over the arching bridge that connected the island of Mount Edgecombe to Baranof Island and Sitka proper. "Benny Johnson," he said. "You went to school with my cousins."

Paul nodded. "I remember. What are they doing now?"

Johnson shrugged. "Addie, he's fishing. Peter's not doing much. Sally got married, has three kids. They're doing good. I see your brother around. Heard he's got himself into some trouble. That why you're home?"

"Yeah."

"Hope you can help him out. He's a good man. "

Dace listened, fascinated by the man's lack of shame as he pried into what Paul was up to. Although Paul didn't respond to the last, she thought he was startled by the assessment of his brother.

"You going to eat at the Bayview?"

Paul nodded. "Still good food there?"

"Best in town." Benny Johnson pulled up in front of a beautiful wood building with large pane glass windows that reached out into the bay. "You say hello to your mother for me," he said as he took Paul's money. Paul slammed the door and patted the roof to send him on his way.

"Come on," he said. "I'm hungry, and you must be starved."

Dace marveled at the beauty of the restaurant. "I wouldn't have expected this here," she said as the waitress escorted them to a table in the bar overlooking the bay.

"Tourism is Sitka's biggest business."

Just reading the menu made Dace even hungrier. She chose a seafood platter that started with a shrimp salad and clam chowder. The waitress, also Tlingit, nodded as she took the order. When Paul gave her his order, she looked at him carefully.

"You're from here aren't you?" she said. "Angela and Deborah's brother — you must be Paul. I remember you, but you were older and ignored us little girls. I'm Susan Adams — was Susan Whitcomb back then."

He smiled at her. "I remember you. Knew your brothers."

"Welcome home," she said as she walked away to put in their order.

Candace looked at him curiously. "When was the last time you were home?"

He sighed. "Eighteen years ago."

Chapter 2

(Sitka. Paul's story. 1996.)

Paul was a week out of high school and trying to figure out what he was going to do next. Not college. He didn't have any interest, and his grades weren't that great. What was the point if you didn't know what you wanted to do? Well, sports and girls crossed his mind, but he needed a job. He had work on the fishing boats lined up for the season just as he'd done the last two years, but that wasn't a long-term plan. He saw what happened to the guys who fished for someone year after year. You worked hard for four months, drank hard for eight months. No thanks.

So he'd put in applications for the pipelines and oil companies. Hard work, yeah, but the pay was really good. And it would get him out of Sitka. God, he wanted out of Sitka.

Sitka had a population of 9,000 and sat on an island with no road longer than the seven miles out to the ferry terminal. The road to the old lumber mill was five miles long, and you could go over the bridge to the airport and Coast Guard terminal in three miles. Newcomers to Sitka called it Depression Drive: drive out to the ferry terminal, back to town, then to the old lumber mill, back to town, and then to the Coast Guard base. If you really had cabin fever you could drive it twice for a grand total of 60 miles. Kitka snorted. He'd been born here. If you wanted to go somewhere? That's what planes and boats were for.

And he did want to go somewhere. Anywhere but the town where he'd grown up. He was tired of being one of those damn Kitka boys. Tired of fights because someone sneered at him or his mom. Tired of backing down bullies who made his kid sisters cry.

Really tired of rescuing Jonas. His brother was two years younger, and he didn't just defend himself, he went looking for fights. All too often, it seemed, Paul had to jump in. And Jonas knew he would, damn him.

Most of all he wanted away from his dad. His dad was a drunk. He hadn't worked full time in years. He wasn't a violent drunk. He didn't hit his mom or the kids. He just drank. And then he'd stagger down the streets after the bars closed, giggling and talking smack to anyone else who was out.

Paul didn't fear his dad. He was embarrassed by him. He wondered how his mother stood it. Of course, that was part of the problem. His father was Tlingit; his mother was white. And no one approved. It was particularly difficult because the Tlingit were matrilineal— who your mother was determined who you were. Who you could marry. He and his brothers and sisters had no Tlingit identity because their mother was white. And no identity in the white world, because no one could see past the color of their skin.

He loved his mom. She was an English teacher at Sheldon Jackson College in town. She wore granny dresses and oversized glasses and talked about books when no one else cared. She insisted all her kids read. Although Paul wouldn't admit it, he actually loved books. They took you places. Right now, he was all about going places.

So, she'd come to the island to teach literature and fell in love with Luke Kitka. They married, had four kids, and here they were 20 years later. Paul figured his father must have been very different when his parents met, but he'd been an out-of-work drunk for most of Paul's life. He wondered what had changed. He wondered if he cared.

Paul stood on the gunwales of boat *Sitka Surprise* as it pulled into the cannery docks at 2 p.m. They'd been out since dawn at 4 a.m. The *Sitka Surprise* was a small operation with a captain and just two crew. They did day runs, putting back in each night. Kitka liked that better than the bigger boats that stayed out for a week at a time. No matter how big the boat, it was too small to spend that much time with six other guys.

He jumped off the boat and onto the dock and grabbed the line to tie it up. He looked up to see his brother standing there. He looked angry, and even more he looked like he'd been crying — or at least trying very hard not to cry.

"Come on, we gotta go," Jonas said harshly.

"I'm not done yet," Paul said evenly. He caught a second line and tied the stern of the boat.

"Paul, Mom says you need to come back now. Dad's...." Jonas gulped.

Paul stopped what he was doing and looked at Jonas.

"Dad's dead," he whispered. "He was out on the mill road this morning waving a gun around, and a cop shot him. Killed him."

The next week went by in a blur of anger and sorrow and downright rage. The hardest part was the inquest.

The cop who shot Luke Kitka was a Swede named Hank Petras. He was about 30, blonde to the point of having almost white hair, even his eyebrows. He wore his hair military short, and his uniform was pressed and creased perfectly. He was a family man, a church deacon, and was known to be a fair, if harsh, man. During the inquest he sat in the front row of the courtroom with his wife, his minister, and the police chief. His fellow officers filled the rows behind him.

Paul and his mother sat in the back row. His mother made the other kids stay home, but when Paul insisted he was going with her, she hesitated and then agreed.

"You're an adult," she said. "You can make your own choice. But you need to be very sure you won't lose it. No matter what the verdict, you have to take it silently. When the judge leaves, we leave. We speak to no one. Do you understand?"

Paul nodded. "He didn't need to kill Dad. Dad never hurt anyone."

His mom agreed. "That's true. But it isn't going to matter. The inquest will exonerate Hank Petras. He's a cop. And the cops take care of their own."

Paul wasn't so sure. There was much talk around town. A lot of the Tlingit community was angry. Everyone knew Luke was an easy-going drunk. What he was doing with a gun out on the mill road no one was sure. He hadn't owned a gun. No one knew where the gun came from. Everyone knew him. Including Hank Petras.

There was some gossip about Hank as well. About the fact that there had been complaints in the past about him being too harsh with Alaska Natives when he made arrests. And about the fact that he'd been in Sitka for five years and was still just an officer. No promotions. No desire to move on. People wondered why. What was he hiding? Who had he been before he came here? Although it was more common in the early 1900s, people looking to make a new start found Alaska to be receptive to that kind of thing. There'd been a mayor of Sitka not long ago, rumor had it, who hadn't existed before he was 40.

So Paul, his mother, his father's father and two other tribal leaders sat quietly in the back row of the courthouse. At the last minute, his mother's best friend Rosemary slid in beside her. She reached over and put her hand over his mother's. His mother grasped her hand tightly, but that was the only outward sign of her turmoil.

Paul was hopeful that his father would see justice, but he was aware none of the other adults felt that way. They were there to give witness to the injustice they expected.

Paul was unprepared for one other part of the testimony — a tape of what had happened that morning, captured by the dispatcher over the police radio in Petras' car.

Petras explained to the judge what happened that morning. Because it was an inquest, not a trial, no attorneys were present. No evidence required. If the judge ruled the death suspicious, then the prosecutor's office would step in and see if charges were warranted. The adult Paul Kitka knew that, looking back, but the teenaged Paul only saw a proceeding where the police officer seemed on friendly terms with the judge, and no one was allowed to challenge his version of the events.

"Got a call from the dispatcher about zero-seven-thirty," Petras said. "People on their way to work at the mill reported that a large man was waiving a gun around at the pullout. One man said he thought he heard shots. A woman thought it might be Luke Kitka. I went out to investigate.

"When I got out there, Luke Kitka was rambling up and down the pullout. I verified he did have a gun and was waving it around, and that he was a danger to society. I told him to put the gun down. He didn't. Instead he pointed it at me. I thought he was going to shoot me, and I fired."

The dispatch tape was played next. The dispatcher, a no-nonsense woman from the Bronx — Paul wondered how she ended up in Alaska — confirmed how the tape was made and started the replay.

"Drop it. Drop it!" Officer Petras' voice said through the crackling of the radio. A shot was fired. Then a second.

The tape was replayed at the judge's request. And then a third time. Paul put his hand over his mother's hands, which were clenched and trembling. Each time, she flinched with the sound of each shot.

Police Chief Hank Campbell testified he believed the officer rightly felt in danger and was justified in using force to resolve the situation. He admitted the commands to drop the gun and the shots fired were very close together.

"Things move fast," he said firmly. "Calls indicated people's lives were endangered. His life was on the line. He did the right thing."

The judge took very little time to rule the death justified. Everyone filed out of the courtroom. The officers shook Petras' hand. The Kitkas were ignored.

"Now what happens?" Paul asked his grandfather.

"Now we bury my son," he said.

"No, I mean, what happens to the investigation?"

"There is no investigation," one of the tribal leaders said. "They have ruled the death justified. There will be no more questions."

"That can't be right!" Paul said a little louder. "You heard how close together those shots were. No one could have reacted and dropped the gun. Dad didn't have a chance."

A couple of officers looked their way. His grandfather shook his head. "It's done," he said. "They have decided."

Two weeks later Paul left for a job on the North Slope, to work for British Petroleum. He got an apartment in Anchorage that he shared with some others who rotated opposite his shift, made new friends, learned to drink too much and successfully flirt with women. After two years, he went through the police academy and got hired on by the state patrol. He couldn't have articulated it then, and wouldn't say it out loud now, but he came to see that the only way Native Alaskans were going to get a fair shake was if they were represented in all levels of the justice system.

He never went back to Sitka. His mom and sisters frequently came to Anchorage to see him; Jonas had found his apartment a convenient escape so he could party away from the eyes that never seemed to stop watching the Kitka kids. But Paul didn't go back.

Until now.

Chapter 3

Dace had no idea how much food was in her order — it just kept coming out. She ate and listened to Paul's story, told with stops and starts as the waitress brought more food, refilled water glasses, and tried to tempt them with dessert. Dace groaned at the thought of it. The salmon she'd just eaten had been stuffed with crab and had some kind of sauce on it. The salad had been enough for a meal in itself. She'd made Paul help her eat it. He'd ordered a hamburger, but she could tell his heart wasn't on eating.

"Anything else I need to know before I meet your mother?" Dace asked.

"Probably, but I can't think of anything," he said as he laid out money for the check. And for a healthy tip, Dace noticed. He flipped open his phone and called his mother to let her know where they were.

As they stood out in front of the restaurant and waited for one of his sisters, Angela, to come pick him up, Dace asked, "Have you ever gone back and looked at the records of the case?"

He shook his head. "I was there," he reminded her. "Besides, there won't be much. When the inquest found the death justifiable, there was no case to be investigated."

"You were there as a teenaged boy," she said, not looking at him. "You might see things differently as one of the best investigators in the state."

He paused and looked at her. "What?" she said.

"That is a very astute observation," he said, turning to wave at a car pulling in alongside the curb. A young woman about Dace's age bounced out of the car and up to Paul. She gave him a big hug.

"I'm so glad you're here," she said. "It's been awful."

Paul had described Angela as pretty, which didn't do her justice, Dace thought, with her dark hair caught up in a high ponytail, big

23

dark eyes, and a figure that showed well in her blue jeans and pink T-shirt. Angela had graduated from Sheldon Jackson College before it closed, married the elementary school principal and spent her time raising eight-year-old twins and teaching math at the high school. Neither Paul nor his mother could figure out where the math ability came from.

"This is Candace Marshall," Paul introduced her. "My sis, Angela Kitka Theron. No girls with you? She's got twin girls," he told Dace.

"If I had them, there'd be no room for you," she retorted, smiling at Dace. "Come on, I need to get you home to Mom. She's held it together for as long as she can, but.... Well, it's been a long couple of days. I wanted her to call you right away, but she wanted to wait until Jonas had an attorney. Seth Jones took the case yesterday, but they wouldn't let Jonas see him until this morning. Bastards. Picked Jonas up Friday at 5 p.m. so that he'd have to spend the weekend in jail. I'm surprised you got here this fast."

While Angela kept up a steady stream of words, Kitka opened the back door of an older green sedan. Dace didn't know what kind, but it was better cared for than the taxi at least. She slid in. Paul put their bags in the far back, and then got in the front passenger seat. "Dace flew us down," he said when Angela paused.

Angela looked at her in the rearview mirror. "I didn't know you were a pilot," she said.

"Just got my license today," Dace said, unable to hide the pride in her voice.

"Good for you."

Angela drove almost as fast as Kitka did, and that said something considering the narrow, winding streets of Sitka. Candace would have liked to have asked questions — was that really a church in the middle of the road? — but there didn't seem to be time. Soon, they were through the small town and headed along the harbor.

"How are you and Jim handling this? And Kristin and Lisa?" Paul asked.

Angela shrugged. "The girls are bewildered, and don't really understand. They love their uncles. Both of them," she said meaningfully. "They got some harassment at school this morning. I've thought about keeping them home, but I hope it doesn't get that bad."

"And you two?"

She shrugged again, and turned east away from the water, and uphill. "I'm furious, I don't for one minute believe Jonas did this, and I think mainly Jim is afraid that I'll say or do something and land in the jail next to Jonas."

Paul snorted. "Have you heard from Deborah? Is she in town?"

Angela parked the car. "She's got an early flight out of Seattle tomorrow morning." She glanced at Dace. "My sister is the only one who left Alaska. She went to the University of Washington for a master's degree in literature and stayed to work on her PhD. Married. Got a baby."

"Jason and the baby coming with her?" Paul grabbed their bags out of the back. They weren't much.

"Not Jason. It isn't easy for Jason to get away — he's an attorney," Angela said as an aside for Dace. "Deborah is working on her dissertation so she's home. She's bringing the baby though."

"How old?" Candace asked to be polite.

"Six months. Paul hasn't even seen him yet, and he's named after him."

"The baby's name is Paul?" Candace asked, trying not to smile. Paul grunted, and blushed a bit. But she thought he was pleased.

"First boy of the next generation. Paul Luke."

Huh, Dace thought. Named after Paul's father, too. He may have been an embarrassing drunk, but there was love in the family. She understood. She'd loved her father, even when his Alzheimer's made him irritable and unpredictable. And she'd never doubted his love for her.

Angela led the way up the steps to a wood-shingled house painted teal that looked out over the slope and to the bay. The door opened, and Dace assumed the woman there to greet them was Paul's mother.

It almost took Dace back a bit, because it was easy to forget with Paul and Angela's coloring that their mother was white. She was a tall, broad-shouldered woman wearing black leggings and an oversized sweatshirt that read SJC on it — Sheldon Jackson College. She didn't have any make-up on, and her graying hair had been hastily pulled back with hair clips.

"Paul!" She came down the stairs and hugged her son tightly. "I'm glad you're here."

Paul held her, rocking her slightly until she let go of him. "Mom, this is Dace Marshall. She flew me down. Dace, Elizabeth Kitka."

Dace held out her hand. "It's nice to meet you, Professor Kitka," she said politely. She had been working at a university when she met and married her husband. She knew professors could be prickly about how they were addressed.

"Elizabeth, please," she said, and rather than shaking her hand, she pulled Dace into a quick hug. "Thanks for bringing my son down here."

They all ended up in the house, done in an Arts and Crafts style with lots of gleaming wood. The furniture was comfortable, and there were books everywhere.

Another woman about the same age as Elizabeth sat in a leather recliner. She was a large woman with careful makeup and hair. She waited with a half-smile on her face.

"Aunt Rosemary!" Paul said with pleasure. She reached up to him, and he bent over to give her a hug.

"Paul, my dear," she said. "Forgive me for not getting up, but I'm altogether too comfortable sitting here."

He nodded at the half-glass of white wine sitting on the end table next to her. "And that isn't the first one you've had tonight," he said, laughing.

She laughed back. "You know me too well." She looked at Candace. "Have you brought a girlfriend home to meet your family? It's about time."

Paul shook his head. "This is Dace. She's a friend. She flew me down here."

"Ah, Candace Marshall, right?" The warmth left her eyes as she looked at Dace. "We read about you."

"None of that," Elizabeth intervened firmly. "Come, Dace, sit down. You've got to be tired. That's a long flight! I really appreciate you bringing Paul home. I feel a lot better with him here."

"I'm not sure what you're expecting me to do, Mom," Paul said evenly. "Jonas needs an attorney, not his brother."

Elizabeth Kitka glared at her son fiercely. "He's got an attorney. And he does need his brother. He needs us to believe in him."

"Mom, you know I stand by you and even him. But Jonas has a hot temper. I have to say if I were investigating this case, I'd look at him seriously too."

"Jonas isn't the hothead you remember, Paul," Elizabeth said. "He's got a good job with Fish and Game that suits him. He's dating a very nice woman who's doing research with Fish and Game. He's got his life together. And what I need is for you to look at the situation as the police investigator you are now, not the sullen, rebellious teen you once were!"

Dace winced, although Paul just snorted a bit. Obviously, Paul's mother didn't have trouble just putting it out there, Dace thought with some envy. Her own mother had died when she was young. She loved her father, but he'd been a quiet man even before the Alzheimer's. And what had passed for conversation with her now-deceased husband was more a series of instructions for Dace and put-downs when she failed once again to measure up. Here it was clear that the family might argue but no one doubted the love they shared. Dace wondered what it would have been like to grow up like that.

"He wasn't that bad," Rosemary said with a laugh.

"Yes, I was," Paul said ruefully. That made everyone laugh, and the tension lessened.

"You said you ate at the Bayview," Elizabeth said. "Do you want something to drink? Seth is coming over soon."

Paul headed to the kitchen, opened the refrigerator and peered in. With a happy sigh, he pulled out an Alaskan Ale. "Dace?" he asked. "Mom, you got any coffee?"

"I'm fine, thanks," Dace said hastily.

"No, you're not," Paul said. "We were up at 5 a.m. to get to Anchorage and then flew down here. So not only has it been a long day, but you've been without coffee for most of it."

Angela laughed, and started running water. "Won't take but a moment," she assured Dace. "I take it you're a die-hard coffee drinker."

"Some people think so," she said, glaring at Paul.

"Everyone thinks so," he countered. He pulled out cream for her coffee and shut the refrigerator door. Elizabeth leaned against the counters watching them with a smile on her face.

"I drink a fair amount, too," Elizabeth said. "Although not this late. Hell getting older. Had to cut back on coffee after supper."

Paul poured the coffee into a mug, added cream and handed it to Dace. She looked at the cup curiously. It was cream with terra-cotta streaks.

"Sitka clay," Elizabeth said. "They were made here from local clay. Pretty aren't they?"

Dace nodded, took a sip and sighed with pleasure. "Good coffee," she mumbled, taking another gulp.

"Life is too short for bad coffee," Elizabeth said as she headed back into the living room.

"Rosemary? Do you want another glass?" Paul called.

"Yes, sweetie, that would be lovely."

He headed in with the wine. Angela looked at Dace and rolled her eyes. "She's not really our aunt," she said in a low voice. "She and mom have been friends forever, and we called her that when we were kids. I am not her favorite. She's always preferred men — even when they're five."

Dace smiled. "She reminds me of my husband's first wife — other women don't really exist if there are men in the room."

"You got it."

The doorbell rang, and they heard Elizabeth open it to let someone in.

"Seth Jones," Angela said. Dace nodded, feeling overwhelmed by all these strangers. Talkeetna was small and when it wasn't tourist season, she went for weeks at a time without seeing a stranger. She liked it — hadn't realized how much until now. She followed Angela back into the main room.

Seth Jones was probably Elizabeth's age, Dace guessed. A squarely built man, also wearing jeans and a sweatshirt, with neatly trimmed gray hair and beard. "Elizabeth," he said, kissing her cheek. "And you must be Paul."

He shook Paul's hand, and turned to her.

"Candace Marshall," Paul said. She mustered a smile and allowed her hand to be shaken as well.

"Let's all sit down," Elizabeth said. Paul tugged Dace into a sprawling love seat, while Elizabeth and Seth settled onto the couch. Angela lounged in a leather armchair with one leg tossed over the arm. Rosemary lifted her glass as if to toast Seth's arrival. He nodded to her.

"So, I've been to see Jonas," Seth said. "He says he didn't do it. Says if he was going to kill the bastard, he'd have done it 18 years ago. Why now?"

"My thought, too," Paul said. "Cops must have had something else besides ancient history to charge him."

Seth nodded. "Paul, what is your standing here? I don't mean to be rude, but we need to set some ground rules before we talk any further."

"I've requested to be on administrative leave until this is over," he said, startling Dace. So that's what he'd been doing before they left.

"But I'm a cop first and foremost. If he's confessed to you, don't tell me. Don't tell me anything that you wouldn't tell the police chief."

"How can you say that?" Angela exclaimed. "He's your brother."

Paul nodded. "And if he killed someone, I'll be the one to read him his rights, and lock him up. But I don't think he killed anyone."

Angela got up and paced. "That's not the point. You have to stand by family, no matter what. You're not just a cop. You're a son, a brother, a friend, a lover," she said with a quick glance at Dace as if wondering which category she fell into.

"Would you cover up for a family member if you knew he'd committed some crime?" Dace said in a level voice. Angela looked at her in silence, remembering the story she'd read about Dace's experiences. "Would you look the other way because he's your brother while he hurt someone?"

Angela sighed and flopped down in her chair. "No," she said. "When you put it that way, no. But Jonas didn't do it."

"That's what I said," Paul pointed out.

"But Paul, there is a lot of gray area here," Seth said. "If he's accused of murder, he may stand trial before he's acquitted. Even if he's innocent. And, even if he's innocent, he could be convicted. Not to doubt my expertise, of course, but it happens."

Paul's expression flattened. "What are you asking me? Would I break the law for him? No. Would I use the law to see to it that he had a fair trial and that all evidence of his innocence was presented? With all of my expertise," he said repeating Seth's own phrase.

"OK," Seth said. "I can live with that. Let me tell you what he told me."

Jonas had been out in the field all week, Seth said. He'd been doing some mapping, checking on some animal herds, and picking up some water samples — common tasks for him in the spring. He'd been dropped off Monday on one of the smaller island northeast of Sitka and was working his way back toward a southwest beach where he'd be picked up on Friday. He was carrying a GPS tracker, and made regular phone contact with the office.

"He loved that part of the job," Elizabeth said. "He liked the mapping part, especially. Some of the land he's been over has never been seen by humans before. He's added names to the maps of lakes and bays. Quite amazing really."

"If he had a GPS tracker, the office should be able to plot out exactly where he was and when," Paul said frowning. "So how was he supposed to be in Sitka killing someone?"

"That's the problem," Seth said. "Hank Petras wasn't in Sitka. He and his buddies are into orienteering. I guess they go out with maps and a route and compete against each other to find all the markers. There's a pool of money for a prize. Never heard of it myself."

Paul nodded. "So, I suppose their route and Jonas's GPS track overlaps."

"Yeah. But here's the baffling thing. They don't have a body."

"What?" Paul asked. "How do they even know he's dead? Much less that Jonas killed him!"

"Right. Apparently, Hank Petras never made the rendezvous site. The guys waited quite a while before getting worried, because people do get lost on these treks. They're joking about how they're going to give him a bad time for taking a wrong turn. But by dark, they're worried, and they set out to look for him. Damn fools, miracle they didn't kill themselves in the dark."

"So, they didn't find him, and they didn't find a body?" Elizabeth asked.

"No, but they found a lot of blood. Being cops themselves, they staked it out as a crime scene, collected blood and called it in. The tests show it to be the same blood type as Hank's."

"But still no body," Elizabeth said, looking perplexed.

Seth nodded, and resumed his story. "One cop hiked out with the evidence from the scene and to alert the chief. The remaining four searched the area. Apparently, they found tracks, followed them, and came upon a campsite that Jonas had used the night before. Thank God he wasn't there, because I'm not sure what would have happened then. However, someone had the idea to call Fish and Game and see if they knew who was out here. "

"And cops were waiting for Jonas at the Fish and Game office when he got back Friday," Angela finished.

Seth nodded. There was silence as everyone mulled over the story. Dace watched them with interest. Their frowns mirrored each other, and the family resemblance showed up. She stifled a smile. Seth sat quietly, letting them think. He must know the family well, she thought, or at least Elizabeth. He seemed to watch her pretty carefully.

Paul sighed. "No body. The charge is murder? Not attempted murder?"

Seth nodded. "The cops felt that the loss of that much blood could mean only one thing. They believe that Jonas carried the body away and buried it or hid it somewhere. Jonas said they kept returning to that when they questioned him."

Paul frowned. "Questioned him without an attorney? Are they trying to get this thrown out?"

Seth shook his head. "He didn't talk, he says. Given the frustration of the police this morning, I'd say he was good about that. Why they didn't call an attorney is beyond me."

"When's the arraignment?" Paul asked.

"Tomorrow at 9 a.m."

"Chance of bail?"

Seth shook his head. "I wouldn't think so. But I don't see how the police even have enough of a case to charge him. The prosecutor must be having a hissy fit."

Elizabeth's phone rang, and Angela jumped up to get it. "Yes," she said. "What? Now? OK, Paul's here, he'll handle it. No. Jonas, that's the way it's going to be, so just shut up and sit tight, OK?"

"Jonas?" Seth said, startled.

Angela turned to the group; her face troubled. "They just cut Jonas loose, said there wasn't enough to charge him, yet, and they're processing him out."

"It's almost midnight!" Elizabeth exclaimed.

"Give me your keys, Angela," Paul said, standing up. Dace stood up, too. "You stay here," he said.

"You shouldn't go alone," Dace replied.

"Why? What do you think is going to happen?" Rosemary asked. "They roll the streets up at dark around here, remember?"

Seth stood up as well, shrugging into his jacket as he followed Paul and Dace to the door. "If Jonas leaves the jailhouse alone, someone will be lying in wait. Maybe more than one," he said.

"Mom? You still keep a gun?" Paul asked. She nodded, and went into the back of the house, and came out with a rifle and a handgun. "Which do you want?"

Dace took them both and handed the rifle to Paul. He checked it for ammo while Dace did the same thing to the .22 pistol. Wouldn't do much, but it was better than nothing. Note to self, learn to shoot a rifle next.

"Seth, you stay here. I don't want to leave Mom and Angela alone," Paul said tightly. "We'll bring Jonas back."

"Really, Paul," Rosemary exclaimed. "Aren't you over-reacting?'

"Given everything? I'd rather be on the safe side," Paul said. He looked at Dace. "Let's go."

Dace was silent until Paul backed the car out of the driveway and started down the slope to the main road. When he turned onto the main road, she finally found the words to ask what was troubling her. "You and Seth, your alarm.... Are you being paranoid? I mean, in a good sense?"

Paul Kitka glanced at her. "If you read any works of oppressed people, you'll find stories about cops who release a prisoner into the hands of lynch mobs," he said, returning his eyes to the road.

Oppressed people? Sounded like university talk, Dace thought. Then again, his mother was a professor. "I know in the South," she began.

Paul nodded. "Out West it was the Indians. South it was Blacks. Boston, at one point, it was the Irish. San Francisco — the Chinese. It still happens. Rarely, but it isn't going to happen tonight. Not if I can stop it."

OK, Dace thought. That made it clear. No vigilantes tonight. She took a deep breath and let it out slowly.

"Sorry you came?"

Dace shook her head. "I owe you, Paul," she said simply. "You saved my life. I'll back you up."

"You don't owe me, Candace," he said gently. "I was just doing my job."

Maybe, she thought. But it wasn't just his pursuit of the real murderer that she owed him for. He believed in her. That belief was worth more than anything.

Neither said anything more. Paul pulled into the police station parking lot. It looked deserted. Paul stopped at the entrance to the lot, letting the car idle while he looked around.

"Over there," Dace said, pointing to a couple of police cars that were idling on the opposite edge of the lot. "Cops park their cars front to back so they can talk," she said. "They're both facing front."

"Yeah. Maybe nothing." He eased the car on into the lot and parked in front of the jail door. He looked at her. "Not that I think you can't shoot, but I suspect I'm better at it. And furthermore, I have a gun permit. So why don't you go in and get my brother while I stand out here and watch?"

Second note to self, Dace thought, as she got out of the car: get a permit for her gun. She heard Paul get out behind her, but she didn't look back.

The lobby was small, but brightly lit. The man she figured for Paul's brother — he looked like Paul, a little shorter, slighter — was arguing with an older white guy with a gut. "I told you, my brother said for me to stay in here and wait until he gets here. And that's what I'm going to do."

"You can't stay in here," the jailor said. It sounded like the argument had been on automatic repeat for some time. "Wait outside."

"Excuse me," Dace interrupted, using a lady-like voice. Both men turned toward her. "I'm supposed to pick up Jonas Kitka. I'm Candace Marshall. Paul's out in the car," she said.

"Get going then," the jailor said. "Just what we need, both Kitka boys in town."

Dace frowned, started to say something, but Jonas gave a quick shake of the head. She turned and went out the door first, partially blocking him as a target. He stepped out of the building, and then stepped out of the lighted door into the shadows.

The cars at the other end of the lot gunned their motors, and one of them came across the lot, pulling up next to Jonas and Dace. The driver rolled down his window.

"Well if it isn't the jailbird," the driver drawled. "And looks like some jailbait."

Dace started to protest her age, but Paul spoke from across the top of his sister's car. "Jonas, Dace, get in the car," he said levelly. Neither of them obeyed.

"And who are you?" the driver said with irritation. Paul didn't say anything. "Wait, you're the other Kitka boy, aren't you? Great. The gang's all here."

"That will be Lieutenant Kitka of the Alaska State Patrol to you," Paul said in the same level voice. "And who are you?"

Candace was focused on the car in front of her, so she didn't hear anyone behind her until hands grabbed her. She fought, using her elbows to aim for his gut, but the man who held her was young and buff, and easily contained her struggles.

"What are you doing?" someone said. "We just want the Kitkas!"

"Grab them all," someone else said. "If we leave one, we'll never get them to the 'copter."

Dace struggled, and she could see Paul and Jonas were fighting their attackers with some success, but there were too many of them. Where did all these guys come from, she wondered. Then someone hit her head with what felt like the butt of a gun, and the whole unreal scene faded to black.

Chapter 4

Angela left shortly after Paul and Dace under orders from her mother. "You've got the girls to take care of," she said. "And your sister to meet in the morning. Go get some sleep."

Elizabeth didn't suggest Seth leave, and he made no motions to do so, looking right at home on her sofa.

"I have something for you," she said abruptly, and headed into her bedroom. She returned with a box. It looked heavy, and Seth jumped up to take it from her.

"What?" he asked.

"After Luke died, I had the tribal elders request a copy of all the records pertaining to his death," she said. "I figured it would all disappear given time, and I thought someday I might want it. I always thought Paul would eventually ask to take a look."

"But he hasn't," Seth said, opening the box and looking at the neatly organized folders. There was also an old cassette tape.

She shook her head. "He put Sitka and everything pertaining to his father in a locked room in his brain. He doesn't go there."

Rosemary yawned. "Well as fascinating as all this is, I'm heading home," she said. "I'm too sleepy to wait for the musketeers to get back."

Seth looked at his watch and frowned. Elizabeth looked at the clock over the fireplace, and then back at Seth.

"They should be here by now," she said.

He nodded. "Maybe they stopped somewhere." He knew it was lame, but he couldn't help but want to ease the fear in her eyes.

Elizabeth found her phone, dialed Paul's number. It rolled into voice mail. Same with Jonas's phone. "Where would they be that they wouldn't answer their phones?" she said. She headed for a closet and pulled out a coat.

"Where do you think you're going?"

"To look for them!"

He grabbed her, pulled her into his arms and wrapped them tightly around her. "Elizabeth, you can't go tearing after them! Think."

She looked at him. "What else do we do? Call the cops?"

He shook his head. "I don't think that's an option," he said. "But first call Angela and make sure she got home safely."

Elizabeth nodded, and swallowed hard. She released herself from Seth's arms — reluctantly — and dialed her daughter's number. Angela picked up immediately.

"What's wrong?"

"Just checking to make sure you got home safely."

"Safe and sound," Angela answered. "Are the boys back yet?"

Elizabeth paused.

"Mom?"

"No," she whispered. "They're not here."

"*What*? Do you want Jim to go look for them?"

Elizabeth shook her head, then said firmly, "No. Stay put for now. Seth and I will go."

"OK," Angela sounded anxious. "Call us if you need us."

Someone knocked on the door. Elizabeth flipped her phone shut and headed to open it. Seth put out a restraining hand. "Easy," he said. "Check to see who it is first."

"I'm not a complete fool, Seth Jones," Elizabeth snapped, but she did slow down a bit as she headed to the door. Someone pounded on the door again.

"Open up!" a male voice ordered. "This is the police. We're looking for a fugitive."

Elizabeth's eyes widened, and she turned to Seth who was right on her heels. She let him go in front. They looked through the front window. Sure enough, two of Sitka's police cars were in front, their light bars flashing. Two officers stood on the doorstep; one had his gun drawn.

"Officer, this is Seth Jones, I'm an attorney for the Kitka family. Do you have a warrant?"

"We're in hot pursuit, Mr. Jones. Paul Kitka just broke his brother out of jail and fled. We have reason to believe they are here."

Seth frowned. "They are not here. However, we received a phone call an hour ago, saying that Jonas had been released from custody. Paul went to pick him up. Something doesn't jibe here."

"Let us in, and we'll search the place. If what you say is true, that they aren't here, we'll be on our way."

Elizabeth's eyes went to the box of records. She moved swiftly to it and closed it back up. She carried it back to her bedroom closet. When she returned, Seth nodded. "You two officers can come in and search for a person," he said. "But there should be not further searching of drawers or such where it is obvious that a person could not be hiding."

"Understood," the officer said.

"First, please identify yourselves. Then I'll open up the door."

"Officer Matt Jameson. With me is Officer George Benedict."

Seth Jones opened the door slowly. The two officers pushed past him, but he was ready for that, and just stepped aside.

"Where are your sons, ma'am?" Officer Jameson asked Elizabeth harshly.

"Seth told you. Jonas called from the jail. He'd been released. Paul thought it was odd and went to pick him up. A friend of his was with him. They haven't come back — we were just getting worried. What does the jailor say?"

"The jailor has a concussion, and he's been beaten. He says it was your sons."

Seth snorted. "Highly unlikely. Paul's a decorated lieutenant in the Alaska State Patrol. Doesn't seem like something he'd be doing."

"Well, blood is thicker than water," Jameson said. "I don't see why the jailor would lie."

"I don't either, but he did," Elizabeth said. "I took the call from Jonas." She watched the other officer as he went through the rooms carefully. He returned to his partner's side. "Not here," he said briefly.

Elizabeth frowned. Something was off. He hadn't really expected them to be here. So, what wasn't here? And where were her sons?

"If you see them, call us immediately, or we'll be pressing charges against the two of you as well," Jameson said. He nodded at them and the two officers left. They conferred with the other officers, and then three of them left in one car. The other car eased up the street a bit and parked where the remaining officer could watch the house.

Seth closed the door.

"Seth, what was that all about? They weren't here to find Paul and Jonas."

Seth looked troubled. "I noticed that, too," he said. He looked toward the closet where Elizabeth had returned the document box. But how would they even know about it, he wondered. He stopped the next thought before it could even start.

"Where are my sons?" Elizabeth wailed. He held her with her face buried against his shoulder. She was tall enough that they were close in height. He rubbed her back gently. He'd wanted to hold her for years, but this wasn't quite the situation he envisioned.

"I don't know, Elizabeth," he said somberly. "I don't know."

Chapter 5

(Over the Tongass National Forest, somewhere. Present day. Almost Tuesday.)

Dace didn't know where she was. She regained consciousness to the loud sounds of a rotary motor. She was lying on the floor, her hands tied behind her back. She stayed still. She was used to being prey with large predators around. Stillness was always her only defense. Her head hurt and her arms were protesting being cuffed, but other than that she was fine. Except that she didn't know where she was. It didn't sound like a plane. A boat? No, there was no rocking from waves. She thought about what had happened, and it came to her. She was on a helicopter. Where were they taking her? Taking them, she assumed.

Without moving, she opened her eyes. It was dark in the helicopter, but as her eyes adjusted, she could see two other lumps on the floor — Paul and Jonas? They seemed to be still unconscious. Probably got whacked on the head harder than she did, she guessed. What she could see of the helicopter indicated it was a large one, without any amenities. Military? Government, for sure. Where would their attackers get a military helicopter?

She could just make out two men sitting on the jump seat behind Paul and Jonas. Including the two she assumed were up front, that made four abductors. Better odds than at the police station. But the odds weren't going to do them any good if the Kitka brothers stayed unconscious.

She felt the sound of the helicopter blades change. Going down, she decided. They must be setting down somewhere. Were they just going to dump them? Why go to all this trouble? If they were going to kill them, why haul them out into the wilderness first? She'd seen some of the Tongass National Forest when she'd flown in. Rugged mountain terrain where only mountain goats could go. Snow-tipped peaks and forests of spruce and fir covered slopes that looked steep, almost straight up. No easy trails there. Some of that land had never been seen by mankind. Dropping them there would be a death sentence.

She felt the helicopter touch down. The pilot didn't turn it off. Instead, the two men in the back jumped up and opened the side door. They grabbed Paul and Jonas and dumped them on the ground. Neither moved. One of the men came back for Dace. She stayed still and limp.

"This isn't right," the young man muttered as he hoisted her up. "I know you're faking it, so listen up. I'm going to cut your bonds loose and then drop my knife nearby. Wish I could do more, but that's not going to be possible. They might leave me here, too, and then where would we be?" He grunted a bit as he brought her out of the copter. "There wasn't supposed to be innocents involved. Most certainly not a woman. Just a cop killer and the man who broke him out of jail. Just justice. Mike said he'd get off because he's Native. Can't let cop killers go free."

Dace wanted to argue with him about the breaking out of jail bit, but wisdom kept her mouth shut. He carried her over and set her carefully on the ground. She felt the ropes on her hands give, and then he was walking away.

"Let's go," shouted the pilot. "Got to be back by sunrise!" The others ran at the helicopter, jumping in as he lifted off. Dace waited until the sounds faded away before she moved.

Her hands were free, and the knife was right there just as the man promised. She sliced through the ropes on her feet. A good knife, she thought with approval. A nice six-inch blade. Sharp. She struggled to her feet, made her way over to the two men, knelt between them, and began working on their ropes. Paul groaned when his hands came free. He opened his eyes.

"You OK?" she asked, while cutting the ropes binding his feet.

He stretched and rotated his shoulders. "Head hurts," he said briefly. "You?"

"They didn't hit me as hard as they did you two," she said as the last rope fell away. She turned to Jonas. He was also beginning to move. She touched his shoulder gently.

"Hold still," she said, her voice soothing. He quieted under her touch, and she sliced through the rope at his wrists. She really did like this knife, she thought. She cut his feet loose.

Paul was up and moving around when she turned back to check on him. Jonas sat up, rubbing his wrists and then his ankles where the ropes had been bound. Dace sat quietly watching them both.

Paul broke the silence. "Well? Jonas, do you have any idea where we are?"

Jonas snorted. "Somewhere in the Tongass. Not that it matters."

"What's that mean?" Paul asked.

Jonas rolled his shoulders. "It's April. We have no coats, no gear, no food, no water. No weapons."

He looked around. It was all rock and lichen. "We're above the tree line — mountain goats live up here, not much else. They can eat the lichen for water. We're not going to be able to do that. We've got hours to walk before we even get to the tree zone. Maybe we'll last one night, maybe two. But we're not going to walk out of this one."

"Gotta try," Paul said. "Can't just sit here and wait for a bear to come by."

Jonas laughed, nodded in agreement. "Yeah, we're not even likely to see bear up this high. But even once we're into the trees, we still have to make it to the shore. Do you know how many miles of shore there are? Eleven thousand miles. We may not even be on Baranof Island. Chances aren't good that anyone will find us."

"Will they even know where to begin looking?" Dace asked. What had he said? Eleven thousand miles of coastline? That seemed impossible.

"Mom will be tearing up that town," Paul said. "She'll have a search underway."

43

"But will they be on our side if they find us?" Dace asked. She held up the knife. "The guy who carried me out of the helicopter said he hadn't signed up for something involving innocents. Just a cop killer and the man who was breaking him out of jail."

Paul grunted. "So that's the story they're using."

"He mentioned someone named Mike," Dace added.

Jonas sighed. "That figures. Mike Anderson. That's the asshole who was giving us shit at the jail. He was Coast Guard until last year. Mustered out here and got married — married the Police Chief's daughter — and went to work as a patrol officer. Those were Coasties who grabbed us. Just doing Mike a favor."

"So even if someone does find us, we don't know if they're going to help us or put a bullet in our brains," Paul finished.

"That about sums it up," Jonas agreed.

Dace sighed. The three of them sat silently, shoulders touching, waiting for the sun to come up. Sunup was at 4:30 a.m. this time of the year. When the sun finally rose, she gasped at the sight revealed. Jonas wasn't lying about where they were. They were high up, sitting on a rock escarpment, and she could see for miles. It was stunning. But it didn't inspire her to want to move. Moving looked dangerous. How had they even put a helicopter down here? How did they know this was here?

All questions that would wait, she told herself.

And at least it wasn't raining, Dace thought, although she knew the rain would come sooner than later. Actually, if she had to play Robinson Crusoe, she couldn't ask for two better companions. After all, this was what Jonas did for a living — with a bit more gear — and Paul could always be counted on when things were tough. She just hoped she wouldn't drag them down. She determined to keep up, no matter what. At least she was dressed for it — jeans, a sweatshirt under a jacket, and good boots. It was what she always wore, and it wasn't much different than what Paul had on. Jonas was missing a coat. That was going to be a problem soon.

As the sunlight brightened the rocky clearing, Jonas was laying out some sticks and measuring angles. Dace looked on curiously.

"He's trying to get a better sense of direction," Paul explained, watching him. "I mean, sun rises in the east, right? But not really. More the southeast. It changes with the seasons."

"So, we don't just put the sun to our backs and head downhill?" she said, smiling.

"Well, close. But it would be nice to know which hill to head down." Paul added, "A GPS unit would be nice about now."

"How about an emergency beacon, while we're at it?" Dace said.

Jonas sat down beside them. "Well, I have a direction," he said. "I'm not sure what do with it."

Paul raised one eyebrow.

Jonas pointed to the rock-crevassed mountain that towered in front of them. "That's west."

They stared at the mountain. "Well we aren't going over that," Paul said. "So what's Plan B? And...Do we have a Plan B?"

Jonas snorted. "Well, we don't have to get to the coastline facing the ocean, just any coastline for a start. So, I suggest we head due east and keep that peak to our back. The good news is I think I know that peak. If it's the one I think it is, we're about 200 miles north, northeast of Sitka. Does that seem possible? Could we have been in the air for three hours?"

"Must have been close to that," Paul said, calculating it out. "We got to the jail at midnight. We were here maybe 40 minutes before sunup. "

Jonas nodded. "The irony, then, is that if we make it down to the shore, we're going to be close to where I came out last Friday, and close to where Petras went missing. Coincidence?"

"I don't believe in coincidence," Paul said. "But I have no clue what it means."

"How did the Coasties even know enough about this place to land here?" Dace asked, using Jonas's term for the young men.

"Part of what they do," Jonas replied. "They fly out, look around. And being young guys, they like to buzz mountain goats. Hence they've seen places like this a lot."

Dace looked at Paul to see if Jonas was joking. He half-laughed and shrugged. Dace took that to mean that he didn't think Jonas was wrong about what 20-something men did when they were told to surveil the coastline.

"Although," Paul said, "coincidence again?"

Jonas just nodded, and then he looked at Dace. "You look reasonably fit," he observed. "And you've got decent boots. You're going to set the pace, 'cause if you get too tired or you fall because we're going too fast, then we're all in trouble. Don't be too proud. If you need a rest or you need a break, say so. If you need to go slower, speak up. We're not trying to set a speed record, here."

Dace nodded, although she knew that the fewer nights they spent out here the better their chances of making it.

"How far to the shoreline if we're where you think we are?" she asked.

Jonas looked at the peak and then consulted some inner source. He sighed. "It took me three days to hike out from the area that they dropped me last week. And the peak is a good deal closer now than it was then. It may take us two-three days of pretty hard hiking."

He shrugged. "Then again, maybe not. It's not like an island is a uniform shape. I can tell you it's going to be a steep downhill trek."

Silence. "Do you think we should make for the lake and your original camp site?" Paul asked.

Jonas thought that over. "Maybe. When we get closer, I'll see if I can locate it. But the shoreline's a big target. My camp isn't. If I had GPS," he trailed off with a shrug.

"What did people do before GPS?" Paul asked as he got up. He held out a hand and pulled Dace to her feet.

"Well they didn't get dumped out of helicopters 200 miles from home, for one thing," Jonas said as he took one last look at the mountain peak and then set out in the opposite direction. Dace followed him, and Paul brought up the rear.

Paul worried. Mostly he worried about the woman walking in front of him with her hair still in a braid — although messier than he'd ever seen it — that bounced against her back as she walked. This was no hike like she'd ever done. He knew she was fit — she hiked around Talkeetna a lot. But there was no trail here.

He wished he had a rope.

The downward climb was slow. Jonas was doing a good job of picking his way down, avoiding the slick lichen-covered rock for the crevices that allowed them to use hands and feet to move slowly down the mountain. But the footing was still treacherous with shale that could slide out from under your feet when least expected.

"Slow down a bit, Jonas," he warned. Jonas didn't reply, but he stopped. Looked around. Dace leaned against a boulder to catch her breath. She rubbed her calves to get rid of the cramps.

Paul met Jonas's eyes. He nodded. Slower. They would need to go slower. Paul looked down the slope, estimating — guesstimating really — and decided it would take them most of the day to get to the tree line. And then what?

He was thirsty. Dace didn't complain — she never complained — but she had to be thirsty too. Thank God for that big meal they'd had for supper. It was going to have to last them for a while yet. But it was water that worried him.

Apparently, it worried Jonas too. He scraped up some of the lichen off the large boulders and handed it to Dace. "Chew it slowly," he said. "It's loaded with water. It's what the goats live on."

She did as she was told, grimacing a bit at the taste. "Will we see mountain goats?" she asked eagerly.

"If we look up instead of at our feet? Maybe. But they're shy," he said. "We'd need binoculars if we wanted to spot them."

Dace looked around. The large boulders were covered with the green film of lichen. Warped spruce grew in the crevices, slowly creating soil pockets out of solid basalt. "You'd think they'd find a more hospitable environment," she said.

"It's amazing how animals — and plants — adapt to places," Jonas agreed. "It's an endless cycle. Fewer predators up this high. They adapt to a place, then they change the place to be more hospitable."

Dace nodded. She pushed herself away from the boulder she'd been leaning against. "OK, let's find *our* more hospitable place," she said.

Later, Paul touched Dace's shoulder gently. When she looked back at him, he pointed. A mountain goat with two young ones still wobbly on their feet were poised on a rock outcropping above them. Dace grinned and gave a thumbs up. Then she started her careful slide, half-glissade, half traverse, down the steep rock face.

By the time they hit the old growth forest, Dace's thighs burned, and her calves were spasming. She knew she needed water. And a flat trail. She stopped just above the grove of spruce and hemlock and looked back the way they'd come.

"My God," she said hoarsely.

Jonas looked at her and grinned. "Wasn't sure you'd be able to do it," he said, and tapped his hand against her shoulder. "Wasn't sure any of us could."

Paul grunted. "Speak for yourself," he said. And then grinned.

An eagle glided across the horizon. Another. Dace followed their path to a tall broken tree, dead and damaged in some storm, where the mating pair had built a nest. She smiled and sighed. She saw eagles around Talkeetna, but they never failed to amaze her. She took one last look at the rock face they'd spent the day coming down then turned toward the dark forest ahead.

"Water?" She asked hopefully.

The underbrush was heavy, and the footing could be treacherous. Hell, it had been a long time since he'd tried hiking in something this — Paul searched for the right word — primeval? It would do. Untouched by humans. Not even a goat trail. He'd like a goat or deer trail right now — it would lead them to water. Neither he nor Jonas had brought it up, but water was going to be a real concern. The undergrowth was wet, the ground damp, but that would be hard to convert to drinkable water.

Undergrowth. He snorted. That word implied some shrubs at the feet of majestic pines. In reality? These trees were huge, not just in height but in girth. Many, if not most, he would not be able to get his arms around. Some, the three of them wouldn't be able to circle together.

There were downed trees, killed by lightning or storms, covered with slippery moss that made climbing over them treacherous. They were in various stages of decay, so that a log might appear to be solid was actually only a shell of a tree. Jonas crashed through one of those, buried nearly to his hips in wet, decaying cedar, and had to be pulled out.

Dead limbs fell on top of each other, created treacherous pockets as good as any snare Paul had ever set. Step in one, sink to your ankle, and it could hold you fast until you pried your leg free. He was already limping from one such encounter. Dace had been light enough to walk over it, or maybe she was just lucky in where she stepped. He had crashed through it, and now he was limping. Bleeding, he was afraid. Leaving blood scent was not good, but there was nothing he could do about it.

Huckleberry, salmonberry, Oregon grape mingled with plants with names like Devil's Club and poison ivy. They slapped back as you pushed through, or at the person behind you. Dace was shorter than he was, and she ducked under limbs that then smacked him in the face.

There was nothing soft about getting hit in the face with Sitka spruce needles.

It was beautiful but it was deadly.

For the first time in a very long time, Paul was glad his brother was along and taking charge. Jonas had grown up while he wasn't looking, he thought with some amusement. And this was his environment. If anyone could survive out here with nothing but a knife, it would be Jonas Kitka. And Paul knew without having to say it that Jonas would see to it that he and Dace survived as well or die trying. Both of them had that protective instinct. They were raised to have it.

It brought back memories to be out here. He remembered his father and grandfather taking them out with their cousins. Learning to hunt, to find their way in the land, to fish. Learning more than that — how to be men. Men of the tribe. And taking care of the younger, the weaker, and the women was a part of that. A strong man used his strength to protect. He could hear his father say that. He'd said it a lot, especially to Paul who needed to protect his younger siblings.

Funny. He hadn't thought about his father except as a drunk in years. Mostly he tried not to think about his youth at all. But now he knew he needed those lessons. If they were to survive out here, he needed to remember.

A strong man used his strength to protect. It was one of his father's favorite phrases. He often repeated it as he cleaned cuts and bruises on his two sons, while their mother shook her head about the boys' fighting. She was a pacifist, she said. Fighting was never necessary. But their dad would just ask them if they had been fighting to protect or fighting to conquer. And he listened seriously to their answers as they stumbled through explanations about why this fight had been necessary.

It hadn't been easy to be of mixed blood in the Sitka schools. They didn't fit. They didn't live in the village where most of the Tlingit families lived. The kids there viewed them with suspicion because their parents rejected them. The white kids viewed them with ridicule. The kids who attended the Bureau of Indian Affairs Boarding School on Mount Edgecombe were even more foreign. They were Inuit and Yupik from remote villages too small to have a school of their own. Many of those kids didn't speak English as a first language.

Three groups. BIA, Tlingit, and white. Paul and Jonas belonged to none of them.

Paul and Jonas had bloodied more than one nose for teasing their sisters. As they got older, Angela had made her own way by being prettier, smarter, and funnier than anyone else. She'd been the first Native cheerleader for Sitka high school. Well, half-Native. The tribe wouldn't honor a Native cheerleader until three years later when a pureblooded teen was chosen. Angela had been in college by then, and she just shrugged. She had better things to do than worry about recognition for cheerleading, she said, rolling her eyes.

Paul often felt like he had been protecting Jonas from himself. Jonas fought. He fought to establish himself as someone to be reckoned with. Paul only wanted to be left alone, and for his family to be left alone. He wanted to be able to go out for basketball — which he did—and not fear his own teammates as much as he did their rivals. He wanted to be able to walk down the hall without having to be always aware of who was around him and what they might try.

Jonas was of the attack-first kind. He got into trouble in grade school because other boys were looking at him, and so he beat them up. He learned to fight and fight dirty. And he didn't wait for someone else to throw the first punch. Jonas punched first, hard and often. He knew Paul would have his back, and Paul did.

Paul could still see that sturdy little boy, fists clenched, mouth tight, glaring at some kid twice his size who had said something nasty about their mother. And Paul would start toward them, knowing Jonas would be swinging furiously. Paul was two years older, lanky with the growth spurt of pre-adolescence, and quiet. He often was unnoticed, or dismissed, until after Jonas started the fight. Then he'd wade in, make sure the big kid got a black eye, and then break it up before any real damage could be done. And then they'd hightail it home before the bully's buddies could get organized. Both of them laughing and giving each other high fives. Paul would never have taken that first punch, but he didn't mind cleaning up the fight. Not at all.

As they got older, the fights got more serious. Both boys were active in sports. Paul was on the basketball team; Jonas had been a state champion wrestler. No one came at them unless they intended to do real harm, and usually weapons were involved. Paul had always been fascinated with knives. He'd begun the collection when his grandfather had given him his first at age 12. By the time he was 15, he rarely went anywhere without one. You weren't supposed to have knives in school, of course, and Paul never pulled one within the building. But at least twice he wouldn't have made it home from basketball practice if he hadn't had his knife and shown the drunken town kids that he knew how to use it.

When he thought back on it, during his teen years, alcohol had been one of the main ingredients in most of his fights. He didn't drink back then, didn't drink much now, but alcohol was a real problem in Alaska both for Native Alaskans and for the gussaks — the newcomers, the whites. Especially during the winters — when fishermen couldn't fish, and lumbermen were in town instead of working in the forests — people drank. As a police officer, Paul was all too familiar with the ravages of alcohol on Alaskan communities. It was estimated that 80 percent or more of all crime in Alaska was alcohol related.

Back then, of course, Paul hadn't known there was any other way. There was no alcohol in the Kitka home, and his mom didn't drink at all. Not that she drank much now beyond a glass of wine. Probably to help his father battle his demons, he recognized now. He wondered what those demons were. Somehow, he knew that his father's death, Jonas's arrest, and now this, were all related to those demons. He felt that vague sense of guilt he always felt when he thought about his father's slide into alcoholism. It was if something lurked in the back of his brain, untouchable, connected to why his father drank. Why he had become the man he became: a drunk, waving a gun he didn't own or know how to shoot, at 8 a.m. in the morning.

Dace was right, it was time to re-examine his past. He thought he could just let it go, let the past be the past. Unfortunately, the past had a habit of not staying put.

"Let's stop for a while," Jonas said, pulling Paul out of his reverie. He glanced at his watch. It had taken them six hours to cross the rock cliffs. They'd been walking for about two hours since they'd hit the forest. That was more than enough for one day.

He looked at Dace as she sat down on a log. She wasn't even breathing hard. Her face was as still as always. He wondered what she'd been thinking about as they walked. He wondered about her a lot. He shied away from that thought.

He sat next to her on the log. Jonas leaned against a tree where he could look at them. "Good to see you two are in reasonably good shape," he said dryly.

"It's water that's going to be the problem, isn't it?" Dace said.

Paul and Jonas looked at each other. "This is Southeast Alaska," Jonas said. "Plenty of water down here."

Dace shook her head. "You don't have to protect me from the truth. I'd rather know," she said. "If it doesn't rain, we need to find water. And soon." She looked up. "And it doesn't look like it's going to rain."

Paul sighed. It was easier to protect people when they wanted to be protected. When they didn't? He sighed again.

Jonas looked at Dace for a moment, sizing her up. Then he nodded shortly. "Water is a problem. I was hoping to cut sign, and we could follow an animal trail to water. But so far, I haven't seen anything. We can go without food. Or we may luck out and be able to find food. But we have to find water soon."

Dace nodded. "If I weren't with you, you'd hunt, wouldn't you?"

Jonas hesitated again. "If I were alone, I'd hunt for food and water rather than trying to get out of here. If it took me two weeks to get home, so be it. But with the two of you along, that makes a difference. And," he paused, then added, "I feel some urgency to get home and figure out what the hell is going on."

Paul did too. He didn't like this whole mess, and he didn't like the fact that his mother and sisters were in Sitka with no one to look after them. Well that wasn't exactly true. Angela had her husband, and his mom was capable of looking after herself. But he worried.

Dace nodded. "I think we need to hole up and let you and Paul hunt. If we had a gun, I could help. With just a knife, I'm better off keeping the home fires burning." She attempted to smile.

"If you could get a fire going at all," Paul said.

Jonas nodded his agreement. "We'll look for a good place to make camp," he said. He started off through the trees guided by something in his head that showed him where to go.

Dace pried herself up from the log she was sitting on and grimaced at her wet jeans. Now she understood why Jonas had leaned against a tree instead of sitting down. Her jeans were already wet from the damp plants that seemed to reach out and grab her as they walked, and now her butt was wet. But she followed Jonas, pleased with his compliment about her stamina. It felt good to be competent, to feel as if she was a partner and not a burden.

It wasn't far before Jonas stopped, seeming to have found a spot to his liking. Dace looked around. It was a small clearing, barely eight feet in diameter. She watched as Jonas walked over it carefully before nodding his approval. Paul must have noticed her puzzlement, because he said, "Muskeg. You've seen it around Talkeetna too. If nothing is growing here, there is a reason. We don't want to make camp on muskeg and come back to find you sank."

Dace summoned a smile. "So, no muskeg — isn't it usually more extensive?"

"Yeah, but Jonas is cautious." There was approval in Paul's voice. Then he laughed. "Which is new."

Dace looked at him out of the corner of her eye but didn't question the meaning of that last remark. She figured Paul was learning to know — and to appreciate — his brother in new ways.

"So why is there a clearing?" she asked.

Paul shrugged. "There may be a rock slab too close to the surface for extensive tree roots to grow down. Any number of reasons I suppose. This isn't much space, even though it seems like it after what we've been slogging through. Sometimes a tree — he gestured to one of the huge spruce nearby — becomes dominant enough to keep competition away from its roots."

Jonas looked at them. "I think this is good," he said. "Candace, are you sure you're OK with staying here while we hunt? Being alone," he hesitated. "Well, it can get pretty scary."

"Call me Dace," she said. "Most people do." They do now, she thought to herself. She wasn't the terrified and timid Candy any longer. She took a deep breath. "I'll be fine."

Dace gave up her knife, somewhat reluctantly. She felt more in control having it on her. The two brothers headed off, and she sat quietly, watching them until they were out of sight, and then, until she could no longer hear them. Their sounds disappeared rapidly Dace noticed. They were quiet men — in many ways.

The forest was quiet. No wind to rustle the trees. No wildlife sounds. A few birds in the distance, but nothing close by. Dace controlled her breathing, emptying her mind. She'd learned to mediate when she was doing yoga in D.C., but it had fallen by the wayside as her marriage fell apart. Now she used it to control the panic that threatened to overwhelm her.

When she felt her control strengthen, and her mind quieted, she looked around. Old growth timber surrounded her, with shrubs crouching at their feet. She drew in a deep breath and pulled in the scent of spruce, hemlock, and cedar. Subtle scents, but they made her breathe deeply to taste them again and again.

She mentally reviewed the day, starting from the early rising of the sun revealing the peak that jutted thousands of feet above sea level in its shades of gray, greens of lichen and moss. She thought about the slabs of basalt, and the crevices that she'd clambered down, sliding in the pockets of shale. I did that, she reminded herself.

She pictured the mountain goats and kids on the outcrop in the distance. And the bald eagles headed toward their nests. And she let the peace the images brought soothe her.

She could build a shelter from the fallen limbs and logs, she thought. The shrubs had whippy branches that she could snap and weave together. She thought of the small huts she'd made when she was a child playing in the woods. Who knew she'd need those skills some day? She smiled at her earliest memories when her mom was still alive, and her father was her hero. She'd shunted those memories away, as she'd dealt with the pain of her mother's death, the bewilderment of her father's decay from early onset Alzheimer's, and then her conversion to being his caregiver. Her marriage had seemed like a rescue from all of that. Now she knew there was no one to rescue her but herself. And in the last year, she'd learned she could take care of herself just fine.

With that thought she studied the deadfall carefully. The large log — almost as tall as she was—would be the backbone of her hut. She could gather wood and branches from nearby and stack it against the deadfall to form a lean-to. If it rained — when it rained — they'd have some protection. And then she'd see about a fire. She could find dry wood and drag it in. Surely one of the brothers would know how to start a fire, wouldn't they?

One step at a time, she reminded herself firmly. And in her mind's eye she could see the eagles soar.

Chapter 6

Paul and Jonas split up soon after they left Dace. Both of them were worried about leaving her. There was always the possibility of a wild animal attack, but the bigger problem was leaving a newbie alone in the forest. If she panicked and ran, they would never find her.

"She's camped alone before," Paul said, more to reassure himself than Jonas. "She'll hold it together."

Jonas nodded, and changed the subject.

"If we're lucky, she's too new to the dangers to truly be afraid," he said.

Paul grunted. "Bear?"

Jonas shrugged. "More likely to be along a stream, and we've not seen any signs of that. As long as she doesn't panic herself, she'll be fine."

Paul nodded. Dace wasn't prone to panic, he thought. She'd been prey. She made herself small and quiet; he'd watched her. It made him want to hit the man who had taught her that.

Men, he amended. Her father, then her husband. He hoped to teach her differently, but for now? Being the small quiet person who let the bigger predators go on by was a survival skill.

"You remember how to flush an animal?" Jonas asked. "You've been a city boy a long time now."

Paul snorted. "Talkeetna is hardly a city. It's barely a town. Sitka is ten times its size."

Jonas grinned at having needled him. Paul smiled unwillingly. "If there is something to flush, I'll find it and send it your way. As noisy as I am, I can't help it," he said laughing at himself. Jonas looked at him out of the corner of his eye, surprised that his barb had missed its mark.

Paul just shrugged. "It's true," he said. "No point in bristling at the truth."

Jonas laughed. "Well, it never stopped either one of us when we were young."

Paul laughed too, and then headed north, gesturing Jonas to head east-southeast. Animals would flee downhill from him. Jonas would have to be fast and accurate with that blade to get something. Paul hoped Dace wasn't going to be finicky about what she ate. It was more likely to be voles or a marten than anything she'd recognize as meat. If they stayed put for very long, he'd try making a snare. He'd been good at it once. He could still hear his grandfather's praise.

Paul made enough racket to clear out the woods for a mile around. Jonas had better get something, because everything would be fleeing, he thought. They'd have to hike out for miles to get another chance. He found a patch of early mushrooms, collected them. Gathered up some greens. Too bad it was too early for berries, even the earliest of them.

While he stalked through the woods keeping in a wide arc that would funnel any fleeing prey toward Jonas, he looked for any sign of an animal trail that might lead them to water. He was troubled to not find anything. They must be higher up than he thought. He'd hoped that now that they were within the forest, they'd find game trails and possible water. Without them, it could mean a fast, dry hike, losing elevation as quickly as possible.

He heard the three sharp whistles that Jonas had always used as a boy, and he turned and headed in that direction. Maybe something had gone right, Paul thought. Or with their luck, Jonas had wrenched an ankle and was whistling for help. He set that thought aside. If anyone wrenched an ankle, it was unlikely to be Jonas. Instead of dark thoughts, he'd best be more careful himself as he slipped and slid down the slope toward his brother.

Jonas had used the knife to sharpen the point of a branch, then threw that to spear a snowshoe hare. He was almost through skinning it when Paul skidded down the last little slope. Jonas looked up from his work. "You're right about your noise," he said. "Everything fled."

Paul looked at him for a moment. He'd been caught up in his memories of childhood when he'd known his brother had his back, and he would always be there for Jonas. But Jonas's taunt brought him back to real time. To the taunting hostility that had existed in their 20s, and finally given over to silence. And he didn't know why. He had told himself he didn't care, maybe even made himself believe that. So, he set it aside, along with all of the rest of his past, and moved on. But now, face-to-face with his brother, he cared. And he acknowledged that he'd always cared.

"You keep trying to needle me," he said at last. "Why don't you just spit it out? Why are you so mad at me?"

Jonas looked at him, stabbed the knife in the dirt, heedless of the harm it might do to the edge. "Why?" He stood up, shoulders hunched, as his barely controlled anger spilled over. "You left us. You went your merry way, living the high life in Anchorage, while we struggled along here in Sitka. Did you ever even consider what it was like after Dad died? You left!"

Paul flinched. In truth he hadn't even considered it. "I was 18," he said quietly. "I was miserable. I had been dreaming of leaving Sitka, and I wasn't going to stay for any reason. I knew if I stayed then I'd never leave, and I couldn't stand that idea. I would rather have died."

Jonas shook his head. Paul's calm tones fueled his anger. "Eighteen is a man," he said through clenched teeth. "You were the man of the family or should have been. Instead you left, and I was the man of the house, and I was 16."

Paul nodded. "I'm sorry," he said. He meant it. It was a long time ago. But he could see that he'd been selfish. He wouldn't change his leaving, but he wished he had been more aware. He'd sent money, of course, but his mom had been the major breadwinner for some time. It wasn't money they'd needed.

"Sorry?" The apology seemed to enrage Jonas, and he threw himself at Paul, taking him down. They rolled. Jonas landed a punch to Paul's nose, and another to his gut, before Paul realized what was happening. He twisted, throwing Jonas under him, grabbed his right hand and pulled it across his chest, using it to subdue him.

"Enough!" Paul ordered. "What has gotten into you? Did you forget how bleak our chances are? Or that we've got Dace sitting back there, depending on us? What the hell are you thinking?"

Jonas glared at him, and then he started laughing. "God, some things don't change," he said between gasps. Paul didn't let go, watching this latest wave of emotion. First the anger, now the humor. He didn't trust any of it. He didn't trust emotion. Not Jonas's, not his own.

"I start the fight, you finish it," Jonas said. "Isn't that the way we always operated?"

Paul slowly relaxed, releasing his hold. "Yeah, but we were usually fighting together, not against each other," he said, rolling off his brother.

Jonas lay on his back looking up at the sky through the tall, thin Sitka spruce. "It was bad after you left," he said finally. "Mom was in shock. For all Dad's flaws, she loved him."

That was one reason Paul didn't trust emotion. What if he loved someone like his mother had loved his father, someone who f-cked up her life? Someone who would f-ck up his life? As a cop, he was often called in to clean up the mess emotions made. Better to keep it light and simple.

Still, he acknowledged, "And he loved her."

"And he loved her," Jonas agreed. "Loved us. The kids at school had new ammo to use against us. The town was icy cold. Mom would come back from buying groceries and lock herself in her bedroom and cry. People were mean."

Paul didn't say anything. He was ashamed. He needed to let Jonas talk, not try to defend himself. If there was any defense. He'd walked away. He hadn't looked back. Hadn't thought about what his family was going through. He'd wanted to be free of all that.

When Jonas fell silent, Paul let out a sigh. "I told Mom I was staying in Sitka," he said. "She's the one who made me go."

Jonas jerked his head up. "What?"

"She said I needed to go, and if I stayed, I would just get bitter and never leave. There would always be something. She said there was nothing in Sitka for me. And she told me to go ahead and leave like I'd planned."

Jonas considered that. "Huh. She was probably right. But you could have at least come back for visits. Why didn't you?"

Paul looked at him. "Out there I felt free. Here? I feel trapped."

"Trapped by us?"

"No!" Paul's denial was forceful, but to be honest, he wasn't sure.

"You know why Angela had her wedding in Anchorage? She was afraid you wouldn't come if it was here, and she wanted you to give her away bad enough that she moved it to Anchorage," Jonas said levelly. "And it doesn't matter if she was right or not. That's how she felt. Deborah decided she had a better chance of you coming to her wedding if it was in Seattle, than if it was here."

Paul looked at him appalled.

Jonas continued. "You didn't come for Angela's graduation from college. Or for mine."

"Shit," Paul said. He hadn't. He hadn't thought it mattered. Obviously, it did.

"It felt like you rejected us as well as this town, and if we even breathed wrong, we'd lose you," Jonas said.

Paul blinked back tears. "I've always loved you all. Really. But...."

"But," Jonas prompted.

"Being close to people means risking letting them down," Paul said, struggling to express the claustrophobia he got at the thought of being too close. "Of them expecting things I can't provide them. Better to not let them get their hopes up I guess."

Jonas looked at him. "You are seriously f-cked up, you know that?"

Paul laughed. "I had an excellent role model in that."

"Maybe you should think about using Mom as your role model instead of Dad," Jonas suggested, and helped him to his feet.

Now that was an interesting insight, Paul thought. His mom was bedrock solid. People trusted her. Students called her for decades after graduation. She'd even won over Luke Senior, and people thought that was impossible. She never seemed to feel trapped by life or find it a burden. Paul set that aside for later.

"Did you want to leave, and didn't get the chance?" Paul asked cautiously, taking his hand, and coming to his feet.

"I never wanted to be anywhere but here," Jonas said simply. "These islands are my home."

"OK," Paul said, glad he didn't also need to carry the burden of that. "We good?"

Jonas nodded. "Yeah."

Paul gathered up the mushrooms and greens he'd dropped when Jonas had slugged him. Jonas finished cleaning the rabbit. There was probably more that needed to be discussed, Paul thought. But not now. This was enough for now.

Dace could hear them coming back. They were joking and laughing about something. She smiled. She had always wanted a brother or sister. She envied Paul coming from a family with four kids. Her smile faded as they came into view. They looked like they'd been in a fight. She scrambled out of her shelter and into the clearing.

"Are you two all right?" she demanded.

The two of them looked at each other, obviously puzzled. "We're fine," Paul said. "You OK?"

Dace rolled her eyes. Men. She'd learned a lot about men's interactions with each other working for Lanky and his pilots. She wasn't sure she'd ever understand them. Whatever happened was over now. "I'm fine," she said.

Jonas had spotted her shelter and strolled over to give it a better look.

"Pretty good," he said. And it was, especially considering she'd done it without tools. "We'll spend the night here. Paul and I found a trail I think will lead to water, but I don't want to head out this late in the day."

Paul swung the carcass from over his shoulder. "Now if we only had matches," he said ruefully.

Jonas snorted. He pulled off his belt and turned it inside out, revealing a small zippered pocket. "Matches, fishing line, and hook," he said, displaying his treasures. "Never leave home without them."

A rare smile lit up Dace's face. "Good! Because I have to tell you, I'm not hungry enough yet to eat raw meat."

It was another hour before the meat — Dace didn't ask what it was, and hoped it was rabbit, not rodent — was roasting on a spit. The three of them sat around the fire quietly. Dace didn't know about the guys, but she had more questions than answers, and voicing them didn't seem particularly productive. Besides, it was peaceful to just sit quietly after the hard day of hiking. The warmth of the fire felt good. A breeze had picked up and the temperature was dropping. She couldn't remember the weather forecast. She'd cared about the weather for the flight time, but she hadn't looked ahead any further than that.

Jonas checked the meat, determined it was done, and swung the spit out of the fire to cool off. He waited ten minutes, then used their knife to cut the meat into thirds. He handed the portions out.

Dace bit into the meat, the juices spurting out and running down her chin. She ignored the juices and chewed slowly. No salt. Stringy and tough compared to the high fat store-bought meats. She had never tasted anything so good.

She finished by licking her fingers, and sighed. "Good," she said.

Paul glanced over at her and smiled. She smiled back. Jonas gathered up the bones and dug a hole to bury them. "No need to attract predators," he said as he stoked the fire.

Dace shivered.

Paul looked at the shelter, it was built like a leaning teepee against the huge downed tree at the edge of the clearing. He faced the fire, and backed into the lean-to, pulling Dace along with him. "Time to use your shelter," Paul said. Jonas had built the fire just a few feet in front so that it would provide heat for them. Except for the initial tug, he was careful to sit close to Dace without touching. She was like a skittish animal, he felt, one wrong move and she'd bolt.

Dace had prepared herself for this moment while she built camp and waited for them to come back, so she was proud of herself for not flinching at Paul's touch. The flinch was reflex, not deliberate. It didn't reflect her feelings about Paul — not that she was sure what those feelings might be. The flinch was from the past, not of the present. She'd all but chanted that as she'd collected fallen wood to build the shelter. Paul's touch was gentle. She moved closer, then reached out for Jonas.

"We're going to need to keep each other warm," she said. Jonas turned to her and smiled.

"You may make the top of my list of people to get abandoned with," he said. He put an arm around her as well. "Most certainly above my sisters."

Paul laughed. "Oh, God," he said, shaking his head. "Remember the time we had to spend a night out in the boat because a storm came up? I seriously considered using Angela as fish bait."

"She knew how to throw a tantrum, all right," Jonas agreed. He settled into the shelter "How old was she?" Dace asked.

Jonas shrugged. "Eight?"

When that story made Dace laugh, the two men vied for telling the best stories of their childhood. She fell asleep in Paul's arms with a smile on her face.

Jonas looked at his brother. "She your girl, bro?"

Paul shook his head. "A friend," he said. As if that were something ordinary. In reality, a friend was something rare and precious. Lovers came along frequently enough, but Paul couldn't remember the last time he'd felt this way about anyone. Maybe friendship had time to grow because they weren't lovers. But now he was afraid to risk their friendship by moving things to something more. That wasn't the right phrase, he thought. No wonder he couldn't talk to Dace about it — he couldn't even come up with the words to talk to himself.

"She's been through some hard times," Paul said.

Jonas nodded. "Figured, from the stories we read. She's doing pretty good out here."

Paul thought about her diaries. When Dace first came to Alaska last year, she'd kept a diary on old cassette tapes. He'd listened to some of them as part of the murder investigation. She'd come to Alaska, figuring to hike until something killed her — weather, terrain, predators. Instead, she'd found some peace and ended up in Talkeetna. Her husband had been a bastard of the first order, and although Dace had never actually said the words, he knew she'd been abused. He frowned at the term. Hell. The bastard had beaten her. Put her in the hospital at least once. The word "abuse" made it generic. He could hear his mother lecturing him about passive voice. He'd been talking about one of his cases over dinner in Anchorage. Apparently, police jargon was full of passive voice. Passive voice means no one takes responsibility for what the verb is doing, she said. She didn't like phrases like... 'the victim was abused'. Someone abused her. Someone beat her. Passive voice put the responsibility on the victim and the bad guy — his mom's phrase — is let off the hook.

He still wrote his reports the way he'd been taught, but he'd started consciously rephrasing it in his head. It made a difference, he found. He wasn't sure he could explain it, but he was more dedicated to finding the bastards — his phrase — when he used active voice.

"I hear you've got a girl," Paul said out loud.

"Yeah. Yeah, I do," Jonas said. There was a bit of wonder in his voice. "I haven't a clue what she sees in me, but I don't question it. She's smart and funny and gorgeous."

Paul laughed. "Enjoy it while it lasts."

Jonas shook his head. "We're going to work on this one and make it last," he said quietly. "Not leaving it up to chance."

Paul was silent. He didn't think he'd ever been that — committed, was the word that came to mind — to making a relationship work. When it was time, he moved on. Occasionally it was the woman who moved on, usually because she wanted a commitment, a family, wanted something he couldn't give. Didn't have it to give, he told himself. But thinking about Jonas, his volatile past, and the determination he heard in his brother's voice, Paul wondered if he was just lazy. Or afraid.

Did he even want that kind of commitment? He liked his life. He liked his job. He liked the women who had been a part of his life — for a time. He never lacked for female companionship.

And when he was 40? 50? He knew men like that. Still chasing after sex. Still uncommitted. Still alone.

He contrasted that to what his brother was trying to build.

And then he thought about his mother and father. And he shuddered. He didn't want to hurt someone like his dad had hurt his mother. Didn't want to get hurt either.

"Do you ever wonder why Mom didn't leave him?" he asked his brother.

"I asked her," Jonas said. "She said she loved him. That he made her laugh. She said she knew he didn't want to let us all down, but something haunted him. And when he couldn't handle it? He drank."

"Yeah. But...," Paul trailed off.

"In sickness or health, in good times and bad — she quoted that to me," Jonas said. "She said that was what love is. That's how she loved us. And he had loved us that way too."

"What a waste of a good man, Paul thought. "Something broke him," he said out loud.

"Yeah. Mom wouldn't talk about what. But she loved him anyway. I got the impression maybe she loved him because it broke him."

"When was this talk you had?" Paul asked curious.

"About six months ago. When I knew Karin and I could have something good. Something permanent. I needed to understand them," Jonas said, looking at the fire.

Paul could understand that. "Do you think their relationship is what made both of us a bit phobic about commitment?"

"Don't you?" Jonas returned. "Both of us are in our 30s, and we don't do commitment. But I want more with Karin. God help me, I want what Mom and Dad had. Good times and bad."

Paul didn't know what to say to that. So, he said nothing.

Watching the flames of the fire, he drifted off. When he woke up again, his brother's head was on his shoulder, and Dace was snuggled between the two of them. It felt right. He stretched his muscles a bit, trying not to disturb the other two, and then went back to sleep.

Chapter 7

Elizabeth Kitka woke up abruptly. She hadn't expected to sleep — too worried — but here she was, curled up on the couch, covered with an afghan. It took a moment to re-orient herself.

She checked the bedrooms to make sure her sons hadn't come in during the night. She didn't think they had, but it was almost compulsive. Not unlike when they were teens. She'd doze off on the couch waiting for them. They'd try to slip in without waking her so they could claim they hadn't been out past their curfews. She snorted at the memory.

She made coffee, watching it drip into the glass container. She poured a cup, added cream. What now? she wondered. She found a notepad and started a list.

When it was 8 a.m., she called the number she had for Paul's office. "Alaska State Police, can I help you?" asked a young male voice. Paul's partner, she thought. He had a Texas accent.

"Captain Wyckoff, please," she said.

"Just a moment." She wasn't on hold long.

"This is Captain Wyckoff."

"Captain, this is Elizabeth Kitka, Paul's mother. We've met."

"Yes, Dr. Kitka, how can I help you?" His voice warmed a bit. Elizabeth smiled, then sobered as she told him what had happened.

He listened without interruption. When she was done, he said in a controlled voice, "Let me get this straight. Someone has kidnapped one of my officers along with two civilians, claimed that he broke someone out of jail, and this is the first I've heard about it?" His voice escalated at the end.

"Who should have told you?" she asked.

"Told me? We should have been flooding Sitka when the cop was killed. I assumed Juneau had a team in there when Paul left."

"Not that I'm aware of," Elizabeth said. "Paul was surprised at that, too, and he also kept saying 'but there's no body.'"

Wyckoff snorted. "So, we have someone charged with murder and no body. And no manhunt called out? There should have been an investigation underway, and a search and rescue team sent out immediately."

"I see," Elizabeth said thoughtfully.

"And now a jailbreak? And it hasn't been sent out to all departments? There should have been a BOLO at least."

"I don't think Paul really broke Jonas out of jail."

"I have not a moment of suspicion that Paul would have done so," Wyckoff agreed. "He is my best officer, one of the best in the state. The thought that any law officer would even think such a thing? Words fail me."

Elizabeth tried not to laugh. "I'm afraid that in Sitka, Paul is just one of those wild Kitka boys."

He snorted. "Well, an investigative team out of Juneau will be there by noon. And I'm going to send his partner down as well. God damn it. Pardon my language, Dr. Kitka, but I can't believe what a cluster...." He stopped — took a deep breath. "I'll send Paul's partner down to supervise. He'll check in with you. Please keep me in the loop, and I will do my best to keep you informed."

"Yes, sir," she said, then hesitated. "Captain?"

He waited.

"I don't think Sitka police can be trusted. I don't know if all of them are involved, but I don't see how this could happen without some involvement."

He grunted. "Nothing has happened in Sitka in 40 years that Duke Campbell wasn't aware of and probably a part of. I'll warn Joe Bob." There was a pause, then a sigh.

"On second thought, I'm coming down. Joe Bob is a fine young officer, but he lacks the authority to deal with Chief Campbell."

Elizabeth closed her phone, drew a line through that item on her to do list. Then she dialed the operator. "Talkeetna, please. Purdue's Flight Service."

"Mom! Unlock the door!" Angela called out.

Who had locked the door? she wondered as she walked to the front door and opened it. She gestured to her phone, and motioned her daughter in.

Jonas's friend Karin Wallace was with her. They trooped past her and into the kitchen.

"Mr. Purdue, this is Elizabeth Kitka," she said. The younger women poured coffee and sat at the table.

Angela gestured at her mother. "Just a moment," she said to the man on the line.

"Dace's plane is still at the airport," Angela said. "We checked."

Elizabeth nodded, and for the second time that morning, she repeated the events of the night before, and listened while a former military man reverted to language he didn't usually use in front of a woman.

"They think Paul and Candace busted someone out of jail? And they can't find them? And the plane is still at the airport?" Purdue repeated, incredulous.

"That's right."

"How stupid do they think Paul is? Where do you think they are?"

"I don't know," Elizabeth whispered. "I'm afraid. I'm afraid they've been kidnapped and dumped out in the Tongass and we'll never find them."

'Damn it," Purdue said. "Let me do some checking. If I and some of my pilots come down there can you put us up?"

"Yes, of course," she said. "But what can you do?"

"Search. The only way to search the Tongass is with lots of pilots. We'll need to get the Coast Guard involved too." He trailed off, thinking out loud. "Let me call you back in an hour. I'll know more then. You talked to Wyckoff?"

She said she had and hung up.

"Are you OK?" Angela demanded. "You never lock the door."

"Seth must have when he left," Elizabeth said. "Karin, it's good to see you."

Karin Wallace was a Native American woman from the Yakama Nation in Washington state. She wore well-worn blue jeans, a flannel shirt over a black T and lace-up boots. Basic Sitka uniform, but she made it look designer class. Apparently in her 30s, she wore her hair straight and shoulder length, and no makeup. She did have on red nail polish, which made Elizabeth want to smile. She and Jonas had been seeing each other since her arrival in Sitka last September. Jonas hadn't said much, but Elizabeth thought the two of them might be serious.

"Have you heard anything from Paul or Jonas?" Angela demanded as she jumped up and headed to the refrigerator. She found eggs and cheese and set them out.

"No word," she said. "What have you heard?"

Angela cracked eggs into the skillet and stirred them. She added the cheese. "Not much. Went by the airport. Dace's plane is still there."

"Cops came by my place last night, looking for Jonas," Karin volunteered. "Said he'd escaped jail with Paul's help. Would he do that?"

"Jonas? Or Paul?" Angela put the scrambled eggs in front of them and poured coffee. Elizabeth cupped her hands around the mug, appreciating the heat, and the smell. It warmed her for a moment. Fear, it seemed, made her cold.

"Jonas I could have believed when he was younger," Angela said with a laugh. "But he's all grown up now. And he'd just had a visit from Seth Jones. I don't see it. And Paul? Paul has always been too rule-bound for that. Besides he's a lieutenant in the Alaska State Patrol. He wouldn't go about breaking someone out of jail."

"Then where are they!" Elizabeth said in frustration. "I keep coming back to the fact that someone kidnapped them. If they are in town, why haven't they called? Where is my car? If they've left the island, how? Where would they go?"

"If they were going to hide Jonas for some reason, wouldn't they have used Dace's plane?" Karin asked. "For that matter, couldn't Paul just request that Jonas be moved to Juneau for protective custody?"

Elizabeth repeated her conversations.

"So fine, we've agreed, none of this makes sense," Angela said. "Where do we go from here?"

A knock at the door saved them from coming up with an answer. Elizabeth peered out the window before opening the door. "Seth!" she said, grateful for his appearance.

"Any news?" he asked. He hesitated, and then hugged her. Elizabeth froze for a moment, then hugged him back, a smile started in her eyes and tweaked at the corners of her mouth.

"Come in and join us. We've been frustrating ourselves by coming up with questions we can't answer." She grabbed his hand and tugged him into the kitchen. "Coffee?"

He nodded, and Elizabeth found him a cup. He drank it black, and sighed. "I take it there is no news."

Elizabeth shrugged. "Dace's plane is still here. We can't figure out why they'd break Jonas out of jail and then not use the plane to get off the island."

"Good point," Seth said. "But then, I don't believe they broke Jonas out of jail. And neither do you."

"Well, no," Elizabeth conceded. She repeated yet again her conversation with Wyckoff. "But why would the police make up such a story?"

"I can think of two reasons," Karin said. "One, we've got more than one group at work here. Two, if they show up here, this allows the police to isolate them and to take them back in custody."

"Door two, I think," Seth said. "Although I find it troublesome that the jailor was given a concussion just to add a bit of reality to this."

"Does he really have a concussion?" Angela asked. "I mean, maybe I'm paranoid, but...."

"That doesn't mean someone isn't out to get you," Karin and Elizabeth chorused.

"Right," Angela said.

"The other problem I see is that Paul and Jonas wouldn't be easy to take," Angela said. "Plus, there's Dace. What would it take to grab the three of them? A small army I'd think."

"Huh," Seth said, as if something had occurred to him. "Well, there is a small army on this island," he said when the women looked at him.

"Coast Guard?" Elizabeth said incredulously. "Now we've got a conspiracy that involves not only the police but the Coast Guard?"

And what would that do to Purdue's search and rescue plans, she wondered.

"Didn't Chief Campbell's daughter marry a Coastie last year?" Angela asked.

"So maybe the Chief had his son-in-law call in a favor. OK. But where would they take them?"

"Could be anywhere," Elizabeth said. They were silent. "Maybe we should go after *why* they would take them?"

Karin sighed. "Jonas and I may have set this off," she said. She told them how they'd put in a record request for any information regarding the death of Luke Kitka, and the deaths in the city jail in the late 1970s.

"I don't understand," Elizabeth said. "Why would you want to know about those deaths?"

"Because one of those men was my father," she said.

Angela poured everyone more coffee and made another pot. "So, who was your father, and why would he be in Sitka in the '80s?"

"I don't know how much you already know," Karin began. "My Dad was an activist with AIM, along with being the police chief in a small town on the Yakama reservation. When I was just a baby, he supposedly hung himself in the jail here. When Sitka police were unresponsive, mom went to the Bureau of Indian Affairs, and then to the FBI. And they couldn't tell my mother anything. Not that the FBI cared about one dead activist in Alaska. Well, two actually. You have to realize that those were tumultuous times for the Bureau as well as the country. There were ongoing scandals, they had been through the Wounded Knee Incident, J. Edgar Hoover had just died, and the misuse of power there was beginning to trickle out into the open."

"I remember," Elizabeth whispered. AIM, she thought. Yes, she remembered them too. American Indian Movement. "Those were bad times here, too."

"So, you're not a researcher with Fish and Wildlife?" Angela asked.

"No, I am. Well, I'm on sabbatical from the University of Washington, and this contract came open. It seemed the perfect opportunity to do some research and see what I could find out about the mystery around Dad's disappearance," Karin said. "I met Jonas, and we started seeing each other. And of course, we shared our stories — both of us with fathers who died here mysteriously."

"Nothing mysterious about Dad's death," Angela said morosely. "A cop killed him."

"Yes, but why?" Karin said. "Did you know that there was never any evidence your Dad actually fired the gun he was found with? No bullets in the gun. No residue on his hands."

"How did you find that out?" Elizabeth demanded. That had not come out in the inquest.

"The Chief said he had no records. Too long ago," Karin admitted. "But the assistant district attorney? He was pissed about the whole thing, and he wrote this long report about the inquest. He's dead now, but the current ADA found the report and turned it over to us. No love lost between the DA's office and the police chief, I guess."

Elizabeth's eyes filled with tears. "I never could figure out why he had a gun," she said. "I thought maybe he was going to kill himself. But he was so against handguns. Hunting rifles, yes, but...," she trailed off.

"So anyway, I think we stirred the hornets' nest," Karin said. She didn't look at Elizabeth. "And someone panicked."

"You should have told me," Elizabeth said. "I have a lot of that information. Although not the assistant district attorney's report."

She went back to her closet and retrieved the box for the second time in 24 hours — a box that she hadn't touched in nearly 20 years.

She set it in the middle of the table. "I suspect there are some answers to our mysteries in here," she said.

"Can't be too many people around who were here in the 1980s," Seth said. He held Elizabeth's hand, but he didn't look at her, giving her time to regroup. "Not many people were here in '96 when Luke was killed for that matter."

"The police chief," Elizabeth said. "He was here."

"And you were here," Angela said to her mother.

"Yes, I was here." She smiled at the memories.

Chapter 8

(Sitka. 1978. Elizabeth's story.)

When Elizabeth came to Sitka, there were so few women on the island men practically met every ferry. Although Sitka had a better ratio than most of the state — the average was 10 to 1 — the Coast Guard station meant that there were a lot of single men between 18 and 30, all looking for female companionship.

She'd never been that popular before. Too brainy, always reading. Perfect for a woman who planned to teach literature. She'd gotten her doctorate in literature, and then accepted a job at Sheldon Jackson College in Sitka. An adventure, she'd told her friends and family.

It took her just a few weeks to realize how divided the town was. There was really a separation between the Native village and the white community. And within the white community, the Coast Guard, the college faculty, and the locals all stayed in their own separate worlds. But at the time there was also a renewed interest in indigenous stories and oral traditions throughout the United States. Elizabeth got involved with the Tlingit Tribal Council in its efforts to collect the stories that had once been handed down from generation to generation.

Luke Kitka, Jr., was right in the thick of things. He'd graduated from Sheldon Jackson with a degree in sociology, and he was excited about a cultural renaissance for his people.

"We almost lost all that heritage, you know," he told her when they first met. His parents didn't speak the language, and he had just recently started trying to learn it. His grandmother was still alive, and she remembered being taught the stories and language as a child.

The federal government gave out grants to collect the stories and record them. Elizabeth and Luke became a team. And, of course, as things go when two young adults spend a lot of time together, attraction flared. He wouldn't act on it — Elizabeth had had to make the first move. He couldn't break that rigid barrier between the white and the

Native community. But Elizabeth had been at the University of Washington, and it had been very different there. Being in a mixed-race relationship made you hip and liberal. Elizabeth was caught up in the romance of it all.

The two of them — the tall, awkward literature professor and the dark-skinned Native activist — became a common sight around the Southeast islands. When Elizabeth wasn't teaching or holding office hours, she'd go out with Luke to some of the remote towns and settlements looking for the elders who would remember stories and languages. She was no linguist, but she was the closest thing they had. And she understood the structure of stories, of teaching stories, and she understood entertainment. And of course, Luke was related to most of the people they met. They collected hours and hours of tapes during the first year she was in Sitka.

One summer evening they were coming back from Hoonah when a storm kicked up, and Luke beached the boat on a deserted stretch of sand. They gathered up some driftwood and made a bonfire. He threw a tarp up on some sticks, and they sat close together under it as the storm blew through. It was late — almost midnight — but still light. Faintly to the north they could see stars starting to come out.

She leaned her head against his shoulder, ignoring the slight stiffening. She looked up at him and smiled. "Kiss me, Luke," she whispered. When he hesitated, she reached up and kissed him softly on the mouth.

She wasn't a virgin, although she hadn't had as much experience as most of her generation. The 1970s were a brief period when women had access to contraceptives and AIDs hadn't yet appeared to scare everyone. But it was Luke's gentleness in making love that captured her heart. There was no aggressiveness, nothing to prove. His traditions on manliness were different. The Tlingit were a matrilineal society, and although men made most of the decisions in the larger world, women often were leaders and story-makers. It made Luke more of an egalitarian than most of the white men Elizabeth knew. And that translated into loving like nothing she'd ever experienced.

When the storm passed and the water calmed, Luke silently put out the fire and scattered the wood. He helped her into the boat. Elizabeth watched him worriedly. Did he regret what they had done? she wondered.

About 30 minutes out from Sitka, Luke looked at her. "We cannot do this again," he said quietly. "The town will not accept the two of us as a couple. Your reputation will be ruined. The college might not re-hire you. And I could not bear for you to go."

Elizabeth naively laughed away his fears. "I love you," she said, blushing a bit because she was saying the words first. "I won't hide that because of what some old biddies might say."

It wasn't the old gossips that Luke feared. He feared powerbrokers of the community, the Board of Trustees at the college, the police chief, and others who would be angry at the two of them daring to cross the lines. And the tribal leaders would be just as opposed. He wouldn't be able to get their approval for the marriage. His family wouldn't approve. He knew of no other white/Native couple in Sitka.

The two of them argued about it fiercely. They continued to work on the project together. And on the trips, they'd argue and then make love and then argue some more. The project moved into phase two, and they began holding language lessons for tribal youngsters who were in Head Start, utilizing grandmothers and grandfathers as co-teachers.

One afternoon, Elizabeth burst into tears and fled the tribal center building. Luke followed her out and found her in the garden behind the building. "Elizabeth?" he asked anxiously. "What's wrong?"

"I want a child like those we work with, Luke! One who has your brown eyes, and your face, and your rich coloring. I love you, and I want a child with you, and you keep telling me I can't have that because of the small-minded views of some people I don't even know."

He held her. And suddenly knew he couldn't deny her this. "We will marry," he said softly. "But it won't be easy, Elizabeth. You must be prepared for that."

"It doesn't matter," she said holding him tightly. "If I have you, and we have our children, that's all that matters."

As Luke had predicted, the early years weren't easy, but Elizabeth was protected from the worst of it. The college president had taken a deep breath and decided to be the liberal his peers in the Lower 48 would expect him to be. He gave a lavish wedding reception for his young faculty member and saw to it that no one overtly harassed her. As Elizabeth got older and wiser, she was very grateful — and loyal — to the man for that. At the time she was too much in love to see anything except through rose-colored glasses.

Her parents flew up for the wedding. They had two, one by a minister in the chapel at the college. A second by the Tribal elders. In hindsight, Elizabeth knew it was only at the insistence of Luke's mother that the elders allowed it. His father didn't attend.

Luke got the brunt of the disapproval. His father refused to speak to him. There was a lot of muttering among his family, his friends, the people he worked with. It hurt, but he stayed silent and didn't let Elizabeth know. He started carrying a knife and made sure people knew it. He didn't leave the house after dark. Elizabeth did the grocery shopping.

Their trips to remote villages stopped. Luke was afraid someone might waylay them, and although he was willing to run risks with his own life, he wasn't willing to risk Elizabeth. Elizabeth's delighted discovery that she was pregnant just months after their wedding gave him the excuse he needed to cancel the trips. Besides, they had more hours of tapes than they would ever be able to transcribe.

He got cornered one night and came home bleeding to Elizabeth's anxious outcry. He refused to go to the hospital, making her fix him up. He didn't tell her that he'd tried to go to the hospital before coming home. They had left him sitting in the emergency room, ignoring him for an hour before he got the message and left.

Things settled down when Paul was born. Naming him for Luke's father did much to heal the breach. Other scandals caught the gossips' attention. By the time Jonas was born two years after Paul, Elizabeth and Luke had become an accepted part of the Sitka world. Not a popular couple. They had only a few friends. But Elizabeth had been right — all she needed to be happy was a family with the man she loved.

Chapter 9

(Talkeetna. Tuesday morning.)

Lanky Purdue was under one of his planes working on a strut when he heard someone approach. He stilled, shifted his grip on the wrench. When a glance at the uniform pant legs of the man standing next to the plane reassured him, he slid out slowly and stood up.

"Captain Wyckoff," he said formally. "What can I do for you?"

"You heard from Dace? Or from Paul?" Wyckoff asked.

Purdue hesitated. He knew Wyckoff by reputation only, which was strange because they'd both been in Alaska for a long time. But Wyckoff was a private man, who didn't seem to socialize. From all Purdue heard, he was also a by-the-book cop.

Unfortunately, it didn't sound like instructions for this FUBAR were going to be found in the book.

"I got a call from Elizabeth Kitka," Wyckoff said. "Professor Kitka said Paul is being accused of breaking his brother out of jail and fleeing. I find this unbelievable. And I have received nothing through official channels about this — something I also find unbelievable."

The man was pissed, Purdue thought.

"I got a call from Elizabeth too," he admitted. "Dace's plane is still at the airport."

Wyckoff looked at him silently for a moment, and Purdue cocked his head waiting for his reaction.

"A jail break, and they don't fly out? What the hell? Do they think my officer is that stupid?"

Purdue grinned. OK, maybe a bit more flexibility than his reputation indicated. "I'm headed down," he said. "Want a lift?"

Turned out that was exactly why Wyckoff was standing in Purdue's hanger. He wanted to hire Purdue to fly him and Joe Bob Dixon, Kitka's partner, to Sitka.

"OK," Purdue said, perking up at the idea of a contract. He was going anyway and taking a couple of pilots with him to organize a search. On his own dime. Having the state checkbook opened would make it much easier. Much, much easier. Gas wasn't cheap. Even in Alaska. Especially in Alaska, a sore point, since the gas came from here.

Wyckoff eyed the old pilot warily. "It's not a blank check," he said dryly.

Purdue nodded. "Noted. But I was going to have to pay for gas out of my own pocket."

In the end, he chose to take two planes, a small two-seat float plane, and a slightly larger Cessna that he used to take tourists out to see the glaciers. That one could carry six plus gear. Rafe would pilot it. He'd pilot the smaller float plane.

What he wasn't expecting was for Elijah Calhoun to show up with a gear bag. And close behind him Bill Abbott, his son-in-law.

"What do you two think you're doing here?" Purdue asked.

Elijah shrugged. "I figure you might need someone to guard your back. And I'm the best navigator you know. Besides you, that is."

It was true, Lanky conceded. Best pilot, he knew besides himself as well, until Elijah stopped flying. Purdue still hoped that would change. Maybe this was a good sign.

"And you?" He looked at Bill.

Bill Abbott grunted. "You're going to Sitka, and you're going to take on the police chief because Dace is missing. I'm your muscle."

Well, he was that, Purdue acknowledged. The joke on the slope was that they saved money on one dozer because they just used Bill to move things around when they needed one. As gentle as he was with his wife and kids, the man was a bruiser. And back in the day before he was a family man, he'd been a brawler.

"Well, get loaded up," he said. "Elijah you can ride with me."

He knew when Joe Bob arrived, because every Alaskan in the hangar bristled just a bit. The young Texan had come up with a whole lot of Texans for the oil jobs. He'd stayed and got on with the state patrol. Turned out he was a fair hand with computer research. But he was still a damn Texan.

Purdue had seen a poster that said, "Happiness is seeing a Texan headed home with an Okie under each arm." Nobody quite knew how Paul Kitka could stand him. But the betting pool on when Paul would lay him out had expired without payout, so people tolerated him.

Purdue put his float plane down in the Sitka harbor and taxied up to a dock. Then he flagged down a taxi to the airport.

The two men watched with some trepidation as Rafe landed the larger plane. Rafe was a good pilot. Purdue had complete faith in him. But the Sitka airport was rated the most dangerous in the state for a reason. Many reasons. Something he hadn't told Dace when he let her head down here for her maiden voyage. It paid to be cautious, but he hadn't wanted to scare her.

"Plane's still here just as they said," he pointed out to Wyckoff as he got out of the plane. "Seems like if they broke a guy out of jail, they'd would have flown off, don't you think?"

Wyckoff looked at the other man sourly. "Especially because there's no way off this island except by air? Yeah, I think the plane would be gone."

Purdue grinned briefly. "Maybe they queued up at the ferry terminal?" he suggested. "Or had a boat waiting for them to take them to, I dunno, where would you go if you're fleeing the law in Sitka?" He helped his men tie down the plane. And then he surveyed his team. Two cops, probably on personal time, he suspected, four pilots and his own private thug. He'd be willing to stage a coup in most third world countries with this team.

But he wouldn't relax here. Sitka was run by three men, and everyone in Sitka would do as they were told. Nice place to live, but he didn't like visiting here.

Wyckoff looked around, headed into the terminal. "We're going to need some vehicles," he said.

"Thomas?" Purdue said quietly. The captain stopped. "You been to Sitka before?"

"Yes."

"And you've met Duke."

"Yes."

"OK then. Make sure those vehicles are safe to drive."

"I was planning on it," Wyckoff said. "I talked to Professor Kitka before we left. She's making the arrangements with her father-in-law. We're staging out of her house."

Lanky Purdue stared at the man's back as he walked away. Elizabeth Kitka's father-in-law? The tribal council was getting involved.

Damn.

He suddenly felt better about their chances.

Chapter 10

(Sitka, Tuesday. Ben Daniels.)

Ben Daniels was having a drink with Duke at the Sheffield House when he saw a Kitka drive down the street below. The car had several big men in it. He took a sip of his scotch — the quality he could afford had improved over the years and it was still his favorite drink. He pointed the car out to Duke.

Duke grunted. "Paul Kitka's boss, Thomas Wyckoff, and Lanky Purdue flew in about an hour ago. They were met at the airport. They didn't come alone either."

Daniels looked at the police chief. He didn't ask how he knew. It was his job to know. That's how they'd divided up the duty's decades ago.

"I told you to leave it alone," he said. "But you had to have Anderson set up some harebrained scheme with Jonas Kitka and Hank Petras. What has Petras done to deserve this? He's been your loyal second for decades."

Duke Campbell took a deep gulp of his beer. "Not anymore. Mike discovered evidence that Hank was going to turn state's evidence against me. It was time to get rid of him. You know he'd collected his 'insurance policy' against me," Duke said viciously. "I needed to take him out first."

Ben did know about the insurance policy and thought it showed brains on Petras' part. He didn't see why Petras would go against Duke now — or how he could without incriminating himself. His insurance policy was a deterrent and a last resort. He frowned. "Did Mike give you any evidence of this?" he asked slowly.

"Evidence! Hank has told me repeatedly that he has damning materials against me. What evidence does Mike need?" Duke exploded.

Ben didn't respond. If Duke couldn't see the possibility that Mike Anderson had his own agenda here, he wasn't going to listen to Ben pointing it out. Ten years ago, hell, five even, Duke would have been suspicious, even if Mike was his son-in-law.

Duke had a talent for picking corruptible men and using them, Ben thought. Hank Petras was a prime example. He would never have guessed that the young man who showed up for an officer's job with his wife and small children would become Duke's hatchet man. He taught Sunday School for God's sake! But Duke had seen something, and he'd made Petras into a weapon.

Not Duke's only weapon over the years. But a long-lasting one. And then Mike Anderson. Even he could see that Mike lacked scruples and could be bent to Duke's needs. The problem was Mike Anderson didn't have the sense to fear anyone. And he was ambitious.

"So then, Mike kidnaps the Kitka boys and some girl and has them dumped out in the Tongass somewhere?" Ben kept his voice mild. "Did you know about that beforehand?"

Duke didn't meet his eyes. "No."

"Stupid."

"He'll learn," Duke said. "Simple is best. I'm not going to be doing this much longer, Ben. Someone has to take my place."

Ben shook his head. "Times have changed," he said. "The days of strong-arming Native Alaskan men because you think you can are over."

"Those two have always been a problem," Duke spat out. "Like their father. Grandfather even."

"Grandfather," Ben said neutrally. "Are you saying Luke Kitka, Sr., has a role in this?"

Duke nodded his head toward the window. "You think that one — I don't know which one of them it was, but it was one of Kitka, Sr., grandsons — would be driving if Kitka hadn't approved it?"

Ben just looked at the police chief. His face was flushed, and Ben wondered how many beers the man had downed before Ben got there.

"You're f-cked," Ben said with no emotion. At this point, he no longer cared about the man's fate. They'd been friends, no that wasn't the right word, partners? Co-conspirators? It no longer mattered what they had been. What mattered was the present. And right now, he needed to take steps to make sure he didn't go down with him. Because it was only a matter of time before Duke was done.

Duke's thoughts must have gone down the same path, because he looked at him belligerently. "If I go down, you go down."

Ben finished his drink and stood up. "Then you'd better figure out how we're going to get out of this one, Duke. Because I'm not going down with you."

It was a problem, Ben conceded as he walked out of the hotel bar. Duke had fanatically loyal officers. He picked them and groomed them, seduced them really. Small acts of loyalty that were in the gray areas of the law. Praise for aggressive behavior with drunks. Well, drunk Natives, Ben corrected himself. Creating an us-vs-them attitude, where us was the 20 or so officers and staff of the police department and them was everyone else. A tight-knit squad, Duke said proudly.

Swede had never seen anything wrong with that, but then he had the same attitude at his fish packing sheds. Or so he thought until the unions came in. Ben winced just thinking about those years. Duke had done what he could — and more than he should have — to help Swede keep out the unions. But the unions — especially with the help of the Alaska Native Brotherhood — had prevailed. The company had been unionized for more than a decade now. It seemed fine to Ben, although Swede was still a bit bitter. Duke had taken it harder than Swede. It had pushed him into even worse anti-Native rhetoric and behavior.

The events of recent years on the national stage had been enlightening. Take a megalomaniac, add in some paranoia and narcissism, and a man could warp everyone around him. And as they careened out of control, they could take everyone down with them.

Ben chewed on that. He wasn't going down with Duke. He was going to retire to Florida. Drink good scotch. Admire the women in their bikinis.

If he could only figure out how.

Chapter 11

(Sitka. Present day. Tuesday.)

The doorbell rang.

Elizabeth started toward it, but Seth held her back.

"Look out the window first," he advised. "See who it is."

She looked wounded but did as he advised. "Two men. I'm pretty sure one is Captain Wyckoff, Paul's boss. I'd guess the other is Lanky Purdue, Dace's boss."

She looked up the street. "Yes, that's my nephew's car driving away. He was sent to get them."

Seth nodded. He picked up Elizabeth's pistol from the table near the door and stepped out of sight. "Go ahead," he said.

"Seth, you're being silly," she hissed at him.

He shrugged. "Probably. But something was off about that visit last night. Until we know what's going on, it's OK for us to be a bit cautious."

She bit her lip, turned to the door. "Who is it?"

"Dr. Kitka, it's Thomas Wyckoff," a man said. "I have Lanky Purdue with me."

She raised an eyebrow at Seth, and when he nodded, she let the two men in. They had to have seen Seth put the weapon back on the small table, but they said nothing.

"Would you like some coffee?" Elizabeth said. "Or maybe something to eat? Did you have lunch? It's 2 p.m."

"Don't mean to trouble you," Wyckoff demurred, but Purdue interrupted. "Breakfast was a long time ago," he said, more at ease with women than Wyckoff would ever be. If you couldn't feed them, letting them feed you helped everyone relax. Besides he was hungry.

Delores jumped up from the table. "Is it that late?" she exclaimed. "No wonder my stomach is growling." She headed toward the kitchen. "Sandwiches coming up for everyone."

Thomas Wyckoff smiled at Elizabeth. "If it isn't too much trouble."

She smiled, shook her head. "We haven't eaten either. I've been telling stories." She gestured toward the table. "A lot of history is piled up there."

"Stories?" he said, moving toward the table. "Have you gotten to the part about your husband's death? Because I'd like to hear about that."

"After we eat," Angela called out. "And I think Karin has a story to tell first. Some of those papers are things she and Jonas have pried out of the DA's office. I want to hear about her father, too. I think he's key to this."

"Your father?" Wyckoff asked as he moved to take a plate of sandwiches from Karin's hands. "I didn't think you were from here."

"I'm not," she said, turning back toward the kitchen for another plate of stacked sandwiches. Apparently, Angela was used to feeding a small army. "But my Dad was up here 30 years ago and never came back. He was killed here."

"By whom?" Wyckoff asked.

"Good question. Duke Campbell, I think," Karin said. "Or at least, he ordered it done."

There was another knock on the door. With a roll of her eyes, Elizabeth looked out the window before going to open the door.

"Father," she said, with obvious delight. "You honor us."

The old Native Alaskan man touched her hands lightly and smiled.

"Come in," Elizabeth said. "I want you to meet some people."

When she reached Captain Wyckoff, the old man — Luke Kitka, Sr. — shook his hand. "We're going to get justice for my son," Kitka said.

"Yes," Thomas Wyckoff agreed. "It's long past due."

"And for the others," Kitka persisted.

Wyckoff closed his eyes briefly, and sighed. "Do you know how many others?" he asked. "Your son. Karin's father I'm just hearing about. Others?"

"Not too many other deaths. Karin's father had a companion with him. There have been a couple of others who disappeared mysteriously during the labor union battles. Many more have been injured, some permanently. The biggest injustices have been to those who have been incarcerated for crimes they didn't commit, for assaulting a police officer when they were the victims. It is time for reconciliation, and for justice. We will not be silent any longer."

"Father, why have you been silent so long?" Elizabeth asked with pain making her voice tremble.

"Because we would not be believed," Luke Kitka said. "There was no one to hear us. But things have changed. In the Lower 48, and in Alaska. We will be heard now."

He smiled gently at his daughter-in-law. "And because of Paul. Paul Kitka is the future. And we will not let him suffer the fate of his father without a fight."

He looked back at Wyckoff and the other men in the room. "We will tear this town apart if we have to, in order to find our justice. The young men of the tribe are not as...." He paused, looking for the right word.

"Isolated?" Elizabeth suggested. "Separated?"

Luke Kitka considered the suggestions. "You are kind, when I haven't always been kind to you," he said. "Yes, we were separate. We saw white men as another force of nature to be endured. We were fierce fighters once. But there are so few of us left. But the younger men? They've been to schools. Taken courses from professors like you, Elizabeth," and he openly grinned at her. "They've gone away to serve in the military. And they know they don't have to allow white men to treat us this way. The Tribal Council has listened to them."

He paused, then looked at Elizabeth, and nodded. "We will have justice."

And for a moment, he looked like the fierce warriors he had descended from — the ones who had once chased the Russians with their cannons and superior weapons out of Sitka, if only for a brief time.

Elizabeth returned his nod.

"We have been telling stories of the past, Father Kitka," she said, after a period of respectful silence that he was due for his announcement — of war really. He had just declared war on the Sitka police. She wondered if Captain Wyckoff knew that. His face gave away little. Lanky Purdue's face was a bit more expressive, and she saw that he did understand. Good. "I was going to tell them about the 1980s. And then I think Karin has a story to tell us. It may not be easy to hear."

He nodded. "I will listen. There has been too much pain because I did not listen in the past."

Someone snickered. It wasn't any of her children, thank God, Elizabeth saw. One of the cousins then, as she thought of them. Although at least one of the men in the room was actually an uncle to her children. He had helped raise the boys, in particular, to the ways of the tribe when their grandfather had rejected them as worthy of learning them. She would always be grateful.

Chapter 12

(Sitka, Alaska. early 1980s. Elizabeth's story.)

There was a feeling of unrest in the Native community. The Native Alaskans here were Tlingit — an Indian group whose heritage was more aligned with the Indian groups of the Pacific Northwest than of the Alaska mainland, who were Inuit — Eskimos, we called them back then. But not the Tlingit. They were not Eskimos, and they were fierce about it.

They were actually a fierce tribe altogether. When the Russians established a fort here, they had to fight the Tlingit to do it. And a few years later the Tlingit came back and ran the Russians off, one of the few successful battles for the indigenous peoples in Alaska. It didn't last. In 1792 the Russians returned, destroyed the Native village, and restored the Russian capital in Sitka.

When I came here, there were plaques about it all. One at the ferry terminal commemorated the Tlingit massacre of the Russian settlers. A second at the Russian fort site commemorated the re-establishment of the Russian settlement, ignoring of course, that the Russians had massacred the Tlingit in doing so.

In 1980, when I indignantly pointed out the racism of the plaques, people looked at me confused. They couldn't see the problem. Ironically, we were at the height of the Cold War, and calling somebody a Russian Commie was fighting words. But our history was skewed toward the white story. Or maybe just the winners' story. It is still skewed.

Although now, we have a small park that tells the story of the early days in Sitka with fewer biased phrases. And the center at the Totem Park has a lot of good detail. But, at least in my mind, there is still a sense among whites of why did those Indians not understand how good they had it with Russian rule? Just because their fishing was decimating the salmon, and their fur hunting... but I'm digressing.

Anyway, the renaissance of Tlingit language, stories, and culture was blossoming. They built a community center, blessed it with the old traditions. And the tribal council was stronger. Pride in your heritage does that, you know.

A focus of that strength became how rough the police were when they arrested Tlingits — usually for drinking, drunk and disorderly, fighting, and, unfortunately, domestic violence. Almost all of the crime was alcohol related.

True for the whites too. But whites were hauled home to sober up, and the Tlingit were thrown in jail and charged with resisting arrest — and sobered up to bruises and black eyes. A couple ended up in the hospital. "Resisting arrest."

So, the Tribal Council drafted a complaint to the police chief and to the borough council. The Borough Council invited the tribal leaders to a joint meeting to discuss it.

I wasn't there — Luke wouldn't let me go. I think he knew there might be trouble. He was there.

The police chief showed up with six officers — most of his force at the time, I think. They stood at attention at the back door, as Chief Campbell walked up to the council, announced he was present, and then proceeded to lay down the law as he saw it.

If anyone gave his officers a hard time, they could expect the officers to use force in return, he announced. "Native Alaskans should stay in the village," Campbell announced. "Stay out of the white part of town after you leave work. Separation will create fewer problems, and we won't have to intervene. But make no mistake, if we do have to intervene, we will do whatever is necessary to keep law and order and to make our citizens safe."

So many problems with that statement. It ran in the newspaper the next day. But I was particularly struck that he obviously considered only the whites on the island to be his citizens. The Tlingit would get nothing from him or his officers. Nothing but more abuse and attacks.

Campbell took no questions at the meeting. The tribal elders looked at each other, and there was a restlessness in the crowd. What now? A tribal meeting would normally be a time when all views were shared, and everyone was listened to until consensus was achieved, or people agreed to think about it and return.

The council knew a borough council meeting would be different, but not this different.

Then Campbell bumped into Elder Mary George.

She fell.

The crowd was furious. One of the Georges shoved Duke as he went to help Mary. And then all hell broke out."

Elizabeth paused. None of the men had moved. There was sorrow on the face of Luke Kitka, Sr., as he remembered that night too.

"Karin?" she said.

The young woman took a deep breath. She looked terrified of speaking to this crowd. Elizabeth started to reassure her, then remembered she had a PhD in biology and had defended a dissertation before a much more critical audience than this. She hid a smile.

Karin began, "My mother is considered a fine storyteller among the Yakama," she began. "I will tell the story as she has told it to me. As if we were there."

Chapter 13

(White Swan, Yakama Nation. Washington state. 1980s.)
When AIM (American Indian Movement) asked Jacob Wallace to go check out what was going on in Sitka for them, he demurred.

"Got a baby girl, here," he said, holding her, with the phone tucked under his chin. His wife came to take her, but he shook his head. He loved to hold her. She was the future of Yakama Nation. She was his precious baby daughter. She laughed at him. He was convinced those were true laughs, even though his wife just rolled her eyes.

He refocused on the voice of the head of AIM. "If I could send anyone else I would, Jacob. But the only person anywhere near you is Andrew Solomon, Lummi. He's too young, too hot headed to go alone. I need you to go with him."

Dangerous to send anyone alone, Jacob thought. And it was true, Andrew was hotheaded. He grinned. They'd had some fine times together at Powwows before he'd married. Now he was a father! That had to come first.

But the future of the Native Americans was at a crossroads as well. Exciting times — dangerous times. AIM was barely recovering from the second massacre of Wounded Knee.

But they were making headway. And the Alaskan tribes might offer a way forward that didn't involve reservations and bloodshed. He didn't understand the intricacies of the legal grounds, but he understood that AIM needed to befriend the Alaskan Native Brotherhood. They were powerful. Primarily a labor union movement, he thought, but they'd been able to establish native corporations that received payment from the U.S. government for natural resources in a way that Indian tribes in the continental United States hadn't.

Apparently even Washington State could learn something following a couple centuries of near-genocide, Jacob thought bitterly.

He sighed. His wife smiled. "You must do this, Jacob," she whispered. "It's necessary for our people. And good for you. You're respected."

Jacob sighed again. He handed his daughter, Karin, to his wife and reached for a notepad. "OK," he said. "Tell me again. Why are we going to Sitka?"

Sitka was not what he expected. He expected Alaska with tundra and permafrost, and instead he got rainforest like the Olympic Peninsula, one of his favorite places to visit. Not to stay, it was too damn wet. No, he liked living in White Swan on the Yakama Rez just fine.

Sitka was lush green, rising up to snow-capped mountains even in June, and dropping off to the bay — Sitka Sound. He couldn't stop looking.

Andrew Solomon was more into looking at the girls. Well, women. They sure as hell better be women, Jacob thought grimly, looking at his companion. They were both getting close to 30. They couldn't be chasing after teenagers. And of course, he wouldn't be chasing after anyone. His wife would have his ears — if he was lucky and didn't take another body part he was quite fond of.

"We're here representing AIM," he told Andrew.

"Yeah, yeah. I can look, can't I? These women are gorgeous."

Andrew wasn't wrong, Jacob thought. They were tall and slender with long black hair and brown skin. He looked at the older women in the village, which was just two streets down by the docks and fishing sheds. They were shorter. You saw that back home too. Better nutrition, the doctors were saying. The younger generations were growing taller. Still, the Tlingits were a tall people to begin with.

Even though it was nearly midnight by the time they reached Shee Atika, the brand-new flagship hotel of the local Native Corporation, it was still light out. Too light to see the stars.

"It's June," their host said, as if that explained anything.

Their host, a man named Luke Kitka, saw their confusion. "During the summer, we get maybe two hours of darkness. Of course, during the winters, it reverses — two hours of daylight."

Luke looked at them as he set their bags inside their rooms. It was a luxury resort style hotel, truly one of the finest Jacob had ever seen. It competed with anything Seattle had to offer.

"Be sure to try the restaurant," Luke advised when Jacob complimented the hotel. "It's world class."

"What's the point?" Andrew asked.

Luke's grin was fierce. "To prove we can. To prove that Native Alaskans can build and run a first-class hotel."

He shrugged. "And tourism is the future of this region of Alaska," he added. "Fishing is getting more and more controlled. The feds tell us when we can fish. Last year? The herring season was only three days. Three days!"

He paused, grinned and shrugged. "Of course, those who have permits made hundreds of thousands of dollars in those three days."

Jacob decided he liked this man.

Luke went on, "Timber? The new environmental laws will protect the Tongass, as it needs to be protected, but there won't be any logging in another decade or so. But tourists? Doesn't look like we'll ever run out of them."

Well, this was what they'd come to learn, Jacob thought. That, and, "Alaskan Native Brotherhood?"

Luke stopped on his way out the door, but he didn't turn back to look at them. "That you need to ask the tribal leaders tomorrow," he said. "The ANB will want to talk to you. We've got some issues. They're about to blow up. We could use your advice."

"Thank you, Luke," Jacob said. "You've been kind to us."

Luke closed the door softly behind him.

Andrew looked at Jacob. "Explosive issues?" he said softly. "Anybody tell you anything about that?"

Jacob shook his head. He was beginning to think he shouldn't have come.

"I heard they were negotiating a union contract with the fish packing plant. Maybe that?" Jacob asked. He headed to the bathroom for a shower.

"Maybe," Andrew said. His voice was troubled.

The restaurant was as good as Luke had told them it was when they tried it for breakfast the next day. Most of the restaurant seemed to be windows that overlooked the Sound. It was beautiful. Yes, tourism would boom, Jacob thought.

He was pouring a last cup of coffee, when three elders walked across the restaurant floor. "Andrew," he said softly, gesturing with his chin. Andrew looked up and nodded. They both stood up to greet the elders.

Jacob didn't know how he knew they were tribal leaders. There was a sense of presence. It was true of his own tribe. He thought if he ever met leaders for which it wasn't true, he would know that tribe was in trouble.

"Elders," he said respectfully.

The three, two men and a woman, introduced themselves. Like their host the night before, the council president was named Kitka.

"Luke is your son?" Jacob asked. The man nodded but didn't say anything else. Tension there, he thought. Family. Same everywhere.

The waitress waited until everyone was seated, then brought more coffee out, and a plate of fresh cinnamon rolls.

"Your leaders said you were here to observe and discuss ways we might partner together. And things we might learn from each other."

Jacob just nodded. Something. They wanted something.

Mr. Kitka gathered his thoughts. Then he sighed. "We are in labor negotiations," he said. "We are unionizing the packing sheds. There is ... resistance."

The other two elders started laughing. And everyone relaxed.

"OK. So more than resistance. Our young men are being beaten up. We had to sue for it to go forward. It hasn't been easy."

Jacob frowned. "I'm not sure labor union organizing is my area of expertise," he said.

"No, no, that we've got under control. The ANB has paid organizers to handle all of that, and after all this time, they're good at it," Luke Kitka, Sr., assured them. "I just explain so you understand why times are so tense. It's the other thing...."

The woman, Mary George, rolled her eyes. "He will take forever to get to the point, and then you won't be sure you understood it anyway," she informed them. "No, we're having problems with the police here. Some of those beatings? Were done by cops. Our young men are getting arrested and beaten in jail over a traffic stop. A couple have ended up in the hospital. The district attorney, he is a good man, but he seems to have no power to stop the police chief, Duke Campbell. The power is with the police chief. And he hates Natives."

She took a sip of water. "So, the city council has agreed to meet with the tribal leaders to discuss the matter. Tonight. But we don't usually have interactions with the council. We'd like for you to help us prepare. And to coach our young men on what to expect."

Andrew looked at Jacob, who sighed. "That I do have some expertise in," said Jacob Wallace, police chief of White Swan, Oregon.

The strategy session took place that afternoon. In the meantime, Luke Junior was tasked with giving them the grand tour.

"What do you do?" Jacob asked as they walked through the national park where the totem poles were. It was a beautiful park and it showed.

"I'm the organizer for the language revitalization project," he said. "Grant funded. My wife and I have been collecting stories from some of the remote villages and their elders. We've got a project going to have the elders teach the language to the young ones in the day care program now. We will lose the language if we don't do something."

"Do you speak it?" Andrew asked.

"Yes, my grandmother taught me. She learned it as a young child."

"And your wife works with you?" Jacob pursued, intrigued.

Luke laughed. "No, she's a professor at Sheldon Jackson College. But we collaborated to get this grant."

"I'd like to meet her," Jacob said.

Luke fell silent. He studied the two men for a moment. "Perhaps," he said. "Perhaps you would join us for supper before the meeting tonight?"

Jacob smiled. "We'd be honored."

Luke hesitated, then sighed. "I'd best forewarn you," he said, "because if you have a problem with it, I'll take you the Sheffield House instead. My wife is white."

Jacob frowned. "Why would that be a problem?"

He snorted. "It is here. Here it's a big problem. You've met my father? He refused to come to the wedding."

Luke shook his head. "Complicated. Not relevant. But it will be nice for Elizabeth to meet you. And second warning, we have two boys. High energy boys."

Jacob relaxed and grinned. "I have a baby girl, Karin," he said proudly. "Six months and she already smiles at me."

Luke laughed. "That's gas, man," he said.

"Not with Karin," Jacob bragged. "She's going to be the future of our nation, someday. Wait and see."

The prep session had gone well, Jacob thought. The team of presenters were knowledgeable and level-headed. His role had really been to give them confidence. Luke, Sr., had chosen good people. Mostly the younger men — although not Luke, which Jacob found interesting — but Mary George was there to lend gravitas. They would do well.

Luke then took them back to the hotel to rest, before collecting them for supper. Jacob liked Elizabeth. She was smart, loved Luke and could cook. What more would Luke, Sr., want in a daughter-in-law, anyway? He shook his head. The two boys looked like their father. Shame Luke, Sr., couldn't accept it.

Elizabeth seemed to know what he was thinking about, and in a moment in the kitchen with just the two of them, she explained, "I don't think it's the case with the Yakamas," she said. "But the Tlingit are matrilineal. So, the boys have no clan in the tribe. They have family — a lot of family," she said, laughing. "But clan matters too, and it bothers Luke, Sr. I see you disapprove of him, and it eases something for Luke Jr., to see that too, but it's more complicated than it looks to outsiders."

Jacob nodded slowly. "Thank you for telling me that. I'll try not to judge."

She laughed. "Well, it's complicated. And it's also true that Luke, Sr., is set in his ways and autocratic. He truly believed his disapproval would mean my Luke would not marry me. But he loves the grandchildren, so he's coming around."

"Children do that," he said, and pulled out his wallet to show her a picture of Karin.

The meeting was overflowing. The council met in the conference center. Like the hotel it was a beautiful new facility with a stage backdropped by curtains that pulled to reveal the Sitka Sound. The curtains were open, and the audience could watch boats go by and seagulls in the air. When the council filed in, the curtains closed.

The mayor announced that this was a special session to discuss "tensions" between the Native Alaskan community and the police force.

Just as the Tlingit representatives filed down through the crowd — Jacob estimated 200 people filled the auditorium — the back doors opened.

"You're late," the mayor said sourly.

Jacob turned and looked. Six cops walked in, followed by Police Chief Duke Campbell. He too wore a police uniform. He had his uniform tailored, Jacob guessed, eyeing the fit. His hair was styled, not just cut, probably the first such he'd seen on a man here. A vain man, Jacob thought, and a man who knew how to make an entrance.

"I have a short statement to make," Duke announced. Ignoring the Tlingit who were about to be seated at the table for those giving testimony, Duke walked up, and took a seat.

An angry mutter roiled through the crowd. His disrespect of Mary George didn't go over well. A matrilineal society, Elizabeth Kitka had said. Coupled with her age? Surely, Duke wasn't so ignorant of tribal ways to treat her disrespectfully.

He started reading. "The Sitka police are faced with challenging times. We are underfunded and understaffed. Like any Alaskan town, we are faced with violence fueled by alcohol. My men have acted appropriately in all instances. If the Tlingit community wants to reduce the repercussions of the violent acts of their young men, I suggest they take it up with those young men. That is all I have to say, and as far as I am concerned, the meeting is over."

He stood up, nodded to the mayor, and turned and walked back up through the center aisle, his officers following. In doing so, he bumped Mary George. The elderly woman lost her balance, and another officer shouldered past her. She went down.

Duke didn't even stop.

The crowd turned ugly in a moment. Jacob didn't see who threw the first punch. He looked at Andrew. "We've got to get out of here," he said. "*Now.*"

Andrew nodded, and the two men headed for the doorway as the council meeting turned into a mob. Jacob thought they were clear, until they exited the convention center. Two police officers were standing there, guns already pulled.

"You're under arrest," one said.

"For what?" Andrew demanded.

"For attacking a police officer, and for fighting in a public place," the officer responded.

"Officer," Jacob began, "we weren't part of it. That's why we left, so that we wouldn't become part of it."

The officer shrugged. He gestured to another officer. "Cuff them and put them in the van. The chief said arrest all of you as you come out. So, we're arresting you. If you didn't have anything to do with it, you can sort it out with the judge in the morning."

Jacob sighed. He hoped his own city council didn't get wind of this. More, he hoped his wife didn't.

He wasn't alone in lockup. Andrew, of course, Luke, and a dozen or more Tlingit men. He wondered if any women had been arrested, and if Mary George was all right. Luke didn't know either, but he was pretty sure Mary George was OK.

"Two officers ended up in the hospital," Luke said grimly. "Three of us, too. But there will be hell to pay for the officers."

"Bad?" Jacob asked. He'd been one of the first arrested, so he'd missed the fight.

Luke shrugged. "Probably not the officers. We had a few with knives, the idiots, but the cops had guns, and batons. Those things do a lot of damage in a mob fight."

Jacob sighed. "Cliché goes, what kind of idiot takes a knife to a gun fight?"

Luke rolled his eyes. "Probably a broke Indian," he muttered.

Jacob snorted. Then he sobered and said softly, "I have a bad feeling about this. If I don't make it home, you call my wife and tell her I love her, OK?"

Luke frowned. "Hey man, that's no way to talk! You watch, the DA will tell the police chief to turn us loose. At most we're here for the night."

He shook his head. "Luke, I am a police chief. Duke is going to find out that I'm poaching on his turf, so to speak, and then that he accidentally locked up a fellow visiting officer. And he's going to be face to face with an Indian police chief. He's not going to like any of that."

"Maybe not," Luke conceded. "But what's he going to do? Bury you in an unmarked grave somewhere?"

Jacob's face was stony. "It happens. All too often, it happens."

Chapter 14

(Sitka. Elizabeth Kitka's house. Present day. Tuesday.)

"I liked your father," Elizabeth told Karin. "He was charming."

Karin took a deep ragged breath and let it out slowly before she responded. Telling the story as her mother, a tribal storyteller, told it, as it must have happened, affected her deeply.

She managed a smile. "That's what mom said, too. He was a good man."

"And Duke killed him?"

Karin sighed. "He didn't come home. Neither did Andrew Solomon. The records here mention two suicides, but there are no names attached. Which was stupid on Duke's part. He could have pretended to put them on the plane home, and the discrepancy would have gone unnoticed. But communication was so much worse than it is now, and he thought he could get away with something like this."

"And he did get away with it," Elizabeth said as she got up, refilled her coffee cup, and gestured in the direction of the younger women. Both shook their heads.

"The next piece of the story is hard for me to talk about," she said. "I've never connected it to your father, Karin, but now I see it must be."

"The DA had been furious," Elizabeth continued. "Furious over the arrests, over the lousy records the jailor kept, over Duke's behavior in the council meeting and afterward. And over the two suicides — men whom no one could name. Nor could anyone produce their bodies. He decided to conduct a formal investigation and impaneled a committee to hold hearings.

"Luke Kitka, Jr., was going to be his star witness.

"And then the day before the hearings, Paul disappeared."

"What?" Angela exclaimed. "How come I didn't know anything about this?"

Elizabeth shook her head. "You weren't born yet. Paul was about four. I don't think even he remembers it. Someone kidnapped him. Said if Luke testified, we'd get his body back. If he backed out, then Paul would be returned unharmed."

"My God," Karin murmured.

"Yeah. The whole tribe went looking. Discreetly of course. The note said if we reported it, they'd kill Paul. Who even thinks about killing a child to prevent an inquiry into mishandling the arrests of a mob?"

"Especially a mob of Indians," Karin said bitterly. "I've been reading the arrest reports. You don't realize how far we've come until you go back and read documents from 30 years ago. A bunch of illiterate, racist f-cks. Excuse my language, but...."

Elizabeth nodded. "Exactly. Even the DA conceded he didn't think anything would come of the hearings, but he wanted to at least embarrass Duke Campbell. He would have gotten state press out of it at least."

"I take it Granddad and the rest of the village had no luck finding Paul," Angela said, looking at her grandfather.

"No, we didn't," Luke Kitka, Sr., said quietly. The lines of his face deepened in remembered pain. "I have never understood how they could hide a child so effectively."

Elizabeth shook her head. "Luke agonized. Here was a chance to make a difference — perhaps — in how policing was done in this town. Perhaps.

"But it would cost him his son. He couldn't do it. He called the DA and backed out. Without his first-hand knowledge of Jacob and Andrew's presence in the jail, the hearing dissolved into he said, he said. With the cops being united, and the accusers having brown skin." Elizabeth's tone was bitter.

"And you've never known who had him?" Angela asked.

Elizabeth shook her head. "Four days. Four agonizing, excruciating days he was gone. And then the hearings wrapped up, inconclusive, and

Paul was playing in the front yard when I went out to get the afternoon paper. Happy, talking about wanting to go see Aunt Rosemary, of all things." She laughed. "And for 30 years, I've wondered who took my son. I mean obviously Duke had something to do with it, but Paul would have been much more traumatized if he'd spent four days with a stranger — especially an angry stranger."

"So, you figure it was someone you knew?" Karin asked.

Elizabeth winced. "Even smaller number. Someone Paul knew. And at four, that wasn't very many people."

Angela shook her head. "Wow. And you all never said anything to any of us? This was why Dad drank."

Elizabeth nodded. "Every time someone else got beaten up by a cop. Or someone was sent to prison unfairly, he'd brood. Hard for a man to feel helpless. Harder, when he could have maybe done something. He knew he'd made the right choice. I know he made the right choice. I truly believe they would have killed Paul if he'd testified.

"But knowing that you had to let go the deaths of two fine men — who he liked very much, Karin — as well as the prosecution of the unnamed men who had kidnapped his son? That eats at a man. It ate at Luke."

Karin blinked tears back. "Luke kept his promise to my dad and called my mom. That's how we knew the story as much as we did. But Mom always wondered why no more was done. Now I know."

"Luke felt he owed Jacob — and your mom — that much," Elizabeth replied. He tracked down Andrew's family too. But it seemed so little."

"Mom appreciated it, a lot," Karin assured her.

Captain Wyckoff spoke up for the first time. "I need Joe Bob to go through these papers, if you don't mind, Elizabeth. And yours too, Karin. If there is anything in there we can use to confront Duke, he'll find it. Breadcrumbs, he calls it." He looked pained.

Angela giggled. Even Elizabeth smiled.

"I'll send him around. You'll know him by the thick Texas accent he has even though he's been here for ten years. I think it's deliberate.

"In the meantime, I want to go visit the jailor while he's still in the hospital and can be found," he finished, with a slight smile.

Purdue sighed. "I'm going with you. I don't think anyone, even a police officer, ought to be going about alone." He considered that. "Make it especially a police officer. Doesn't look like Paul is the first officer Duke has disappeared."

Luke Kitka looked at them. "We have drivers to take you where you're needed. We're with you every step of the way."

Chapter 15

(Sitka. Present Day. Still Tuesday.)

Wyckoff was in the passenger seat. One of Paul's many cousins was driving. Purdue looked out at the town from the back seat as they headed up to the hospital. It was a pretty town, he thought.

"So, do you believe her story? You think Duke killed a couple of men because one was a cop?" he asked.

Wyckoff hesitated. "Hard to dispute it, since I'm missing another cop right now," he said finally.

Purdue snorted. "True. Native cops it looks like."

The other man sighed. "We've got real problems in this state. I assume you've read the newspaper articles?"

Purdue had. Some remote villages had no local cops. Others paid so little, only men with criminal records applied — including sexual assault convictions. The *Anchorage Daily News* had won a Pulitzer for their reporting on the issue. Deservedly. After that, more money was supplied to the state patrol for more officers. More oversight. Purdue wasn't sure it was going to make a difference.

"Add in Black Lives Matter calling attention to police brutality toward non-whites in the Lower 48?" Wyckoff said. "Did you know police shootings are higher among Native Americans than in the Black communities? True nationwide. Most certainly true here."

The Kitka who was driving looked over at Wyckoff but didn't say anything. He pulled into the parking lot and shut off the car.

Wyckoff turned and looked at Purdue over the seat. "So yes. I believe Sitka has had a history of beating up Alaska Natives, if for no other reason than it's true everywhere."

Purdue nodded. "And then you add in Duke Campbell."

Wyckoff opened the car door. "And then you add in Duke Campbell."

He hesitated. "I have had hopes that Paul Kitka could be the solution to Alaska's problems someday."

"Paul?" Purdue asked. "How so?"

"A highly regarded, well trained, thoughtful Alaskan Native state patrol officer? He could go all the way to the top. But so far, he seems content to be a lieutenant with a high solve rate and a comfortable lifestyle. I keep hoping to see signs of ambition, but so far that's lacking. It would require commitment and passion on his part. And he doesn't do commitment — publicly or privately, as he's fond of telling the women who pursue him." Wyckoff rolled his eyes. Paul's dating life was gossip material among his officers. "But he could be the solution to at least part of the issues we face as a state."

Purdue got out the car and started walking toward the hospital. "If a bunch of f-cking racist cops don't kill him."

Wyckoff closed his eyes briefly and nodded. "Yeah. If a bunch of f-cking racist cops don't kill him," he repeated.

Purdue waited in the hallway with the local officer who stood guard. Their driver had stayed with the car. No one was taking chances, it seemed.

The local officer hadn't been happy about Captain Wyckoff going in to see the jailor, but he obviously knew protesting wasn't going to help him in any way. Wyckoff barely paused for the cop's permission before pushing open the door and entering the room.

He looked at the man in the hospital bed. He had obviously been beaten. The doctors said he had a concussion.

He was a big man who had gone to fat around the middle. Wyckoff studied him a moment. The man closed his eyes.

"So why don't you tell me what happened?" Wyckoff said, after identifying himself.

The man didn't say anything.

"You might as well tell me the story," he said. "Sooner or later you will have to. Sooner would be good, so I can send you to Juneau in protective custody."

The man opened his eyes and looked at him puzzled.

"Or, I can walk out the door, and tell Duke you've told me everything and see what happens."

"I haven't told you anything," he protested.

Wyckoff waited for the man to work it through. He could see when he got it. He paled.

"Shit."

Wyckoff smiled. It wasn't friendly.

"So, what happened?"

And this time the jailor told him.

Mike Anderson had come through the jailhouse door with a swagger. "That's taken care of," he said.

The jailor had looked at him and shook his head. "You're making it overly complicated, Mike. Should have just shot them and let them lie."

Mike shrugged. "If they just disappear, it's easier. Really, who's going to challenge the story that a Kitka brother broke the other one out of jail?"

The jailor looked at him. "Yeah? And just how did he do that? With me standing here?"

Mike smiled slowly. "Well that's a good question, isn't it?"

Mike Anderson was 32, fit, and an experienced brawler. The jailor was 55 and hadn't thrown a punch in 30 years. He'd gone down without even connecting. He'd blacked out to Anderson kicking him methodically with steeled toed shoes.

Wyckoff looked at him. "So, you were advocating killing a State Patrol officer?"

The jailor closed his eyes. "He's not a State Patrol officer in this town, Captain," he said wearily. "He's a Kitka."

Wyckoff looked at him. "You'll be facing charges as a co-conspira-tor," he said. "However, I'll put in a word with the ADA. But you're fin-ished with police work. I suggest you think about what you'll do next."

Wyckoff walked out the door.

"Captain?" the jailor — ex-jailor — said. "Who was the girl?"

Wyckoff looked back. "You're just asking that now? She was a pilot on her first solo flight, giving a friend a ride to Sitka. Her boss is Lanky Purdue."

The man's face paled. Lanky had a reputation among the old sour-doughs in the state. He'd been here a long time.

Wyckoff nodded. "I'd stay in here until the Juneau State Patrol of-ficers come to take you into custody. If Duke doesn't get you, Lanky might."

Chapter 16

(Sitka. Elizabeth's home. Still Tuesday.)

Joe Bob listened to his boss on the phone. He pulled his ear away from it and looked at it in bafflement. His boss had gone to the Sitka police department after leaving the hospital to see Duke Campbell and demand an investigation into the disappearance of his officer. Joe Bob would like to have been a fly on the wall for that conversation. Although, apparently Duke had ducked out, leaving the dispatcher to handle the irate captain. The assistant chief Mike Anderson hadn't been available either. Fancy that. The dispatcher had been more than willing to find the captain a desk and to pull whatever records he wanted. Duke might regret leaving his office unguarded.

Maybe Lanky could be prevailed upon to divulge the details.

"What?" Elijah Calhoun said. He looked up from his seat on the floor. He held a paper plate with chicken and potato salad on it and watched the crowd at Elizabeth Kitka's home. The lawyer Seth Jones was pretty much glued to her side. Elijah would make book that Seth wasn't going home tonight. Well, good for her. Elijah thought Elizabeth was a pretty amazing woman. Maybe she'd get a second chance at love. She deserved it. A voice in his head asked if maybe he deserved it too, and he shut it down. No. No, he didn't.

Women from the various Kitka households had shown up at 7 p.m. bearing food. Unlike the men, who tended to be quiet because of the elder Kitka's presence, the women laughed and joked in the kitchen with Elizabeth and her daughters. At some point another daughter had arrived from Seattle, bearing a little boy, Paul Luke Kitka. His great-grandfather was holding him, quite competently, Elijah noted. His heart clenched for a moment at the reminder of his own child's death. He set the pain aside. In the last few years, he'd gotten used to the reminders and to the pain.

"I think my boss is asking me to go drinking at the 3 1/2 Mile Club tonight," Joe Bob was saying when he looked up again.

Elijah laughed, spitting out his drink. "Does he know what kind of bar that is?"

"No?" Joe Bob guessed. The 3 1/2 Mile Club — named because it was 3 1/2 miles out of town — was notorious. But he didn't think Andrew Wyckoff was, or had ever been, the kind of man who would know about sleazy dives in out-of-the-way places.

Bill Abbott grunted. "Bet he does. That's why he's sending you."

"And me," Elijah said. "You're not going alone."

"And me," said Rafe.

The other men looked at him, consideringly.

"What?"

"Are you even old enough to go into a bar?" Elijah asked.

Rafe threw his napkin at him.

Joe Bob took Captain Wyckoff off hold. "Rafe and Elijah say they'll go with me," he said.

"Good," Wyckoff said, proving he did indeed know about seedy dives in small Alaska towns. "Tell Bill I've got another job for him this evening."

Abbott snorted. "You just don't want to have to explain to my wife why you sent me into a titty bar in Sitka."

"That too," Wyckoff said, over the top of the exclamations from the younger men.

Abbott looked at them. "You didn't know the 3 1/2 Mile Club is a titty bar?" he asked.

Rafe shook his head, a bit wide-eyed. "Maybe I'm not old enough to go along after all?"

Elijah's smile was wicked. "This will be fun."

All the men who had flown in from Talkeetna had hotel rooms at the Shee Atika, complements of the tribal corporation. It was by far the nicest place any of the three young men had ever stayed in.

Turned out Elijah's notion of bar crawl attire was snug jeans, a black T shirt, and low boots that had seen better days. The same thing he wore most days.

Joe Bob frowned. "That's what you're wearing?"

Elijah laughed. "We're not going to pick up women at the 3 1/2 Mile Club," he said. "Men go there to watch women strip, get served by women wearing next to nothing, and get drunk on over-priced, watered down drinks. Women don't go there much."

Rafe nodded, chose similar clothes, although his T-shirt said, "I'd tell you I'm a crazy Alaskan pilot. But that's redundant."

Elijah nodded approvingly. "Good. The Coasties ought to like that one."

Joe Bob sighed. "I didn't bring any of my Texas T-shirts," he whined.

Rafe's eyes widened. "We're trying to get them to talk to us, not start a bar fight," he said.

Joe Bob laughed. "Just kidding." Turned out the only T-shirts he'd brought along were gray work out T-shirts. He'd expected to be wearing his uniform most of the time.

Elijah looked at the two younger men with narrowed eyes. "Look, we do not want to get into a fight," he warned. "Getting tossed in jail here appears to be dangerous."

He looked at Joe Bob. "Especially for police officers."

Joe Bob sobered. "Just kidding around," he said. "I'm an off-duty police officer. My boss is in town with me. Believe me, it isn't jail that I'm afraid of. You have met my boss, haven't you?"

Elijah smiled at that. "You just remember that."

The 3 1/2 Mile Club was the google-definition of a seedy bar. Even on a Tuesday night, when they pulled in at 10 p.m. the parking lot was full of pickups, SUVs, and old-fashioned open-sided jeeps. The building was one story, made of unpainted wood and built up a bit on stilts. It backed up against the hillside and looked out across the road to the harbor. Not that anyone inside could see that from inside — no windows. Neon beer lights lined up along the front on both sides of the front door. A big burly man stood in front talking to a couple of fit young men. Coasties.

Elijah turned off the engine. "One last thing, do not make any disparaging remarks about the women."

"Why? They going to be old and sad?" Joe Bob asked.

"To the contrary. You won't find a bar like this anywhere else. It's seedy, but the dancers and waitresses are all bored wives of the Coast Guard sailors."

"What?" said Rafe and Joe Bob at the same time.

"True story. Coast Guard sailors are out for two weeks at a time. And some of their wives dance here."

Rafe frowned. "But that means their husbands' buddies are watching their wives strip? How does that work?"

Elijah shrugged. "I don't understand it either. But then, their wives dance too — when they're out to sea."

"That's got to be an urban myth," Joe Bob objected.

Elijah shrugged again. "Don't know if it's true. Just don't criticize the dancers and be nice to the waitresses. That could be her husband's best friend sitting at the next table. Or her best friend's husband. Sitka is a damn small town."

The bouncer checked their IDs, frowned suspiciously at Rafe, but handed his ID back to him. He wouldn't be the first young guy getting into the Club with ID whose ink was barely dry. It was a Coast Guard bar in a Coast Guard town. Look too carefully and you'd be kicking out half your clientele.

"Am I going to be the only non-white in here?" Rafe murmured as they stepped into the bar.

"Shit, I didn't think of that," Joe Bob admitted. None of the Kitka men had been willing to go along. You're on your own for that one, they'd said.

"Too late to worry about it now," Elijah said with a shrug. "But the Coast Guard is far from all white, and money talks."

They stood for a moment, letting their eyes adjust to the nearly dark room, and looking for a table. Elijah nodded toward one off to the left and toward the back. The place was packed. He'd guessed wrong about the time things would start up. These boys had been here for a couple of hours and were already exuberantly cheering the dancers. Bar didn't close until 2 a.m.

Elijah grinned. Alaskans were famous for their hard-drinking bars. It had been much worse when he first started flying, which was why he knew the stories of places like Sitka and the 3 1/2 Mile Club. At one point, the average consumption of alcohol was over a gallon a month for every man, woman and child in the state. Bars stayed open until 4 a.m. and then switched and served breakfast until 6 a.m. when it was legal to serve alcohol again.

In a state where there were ten men for every woman, alcohol was a man's next best friend. It was also related to 80 percent of the domestic violence, and probably that much of other crime.

When he'd been Rafe's age, he could party with the best of them. Then he married, settled down, had kids.

One crash landing later, he had lost it all. Wasn't his fault, everyone said so. Didn't matter. They were gone, and he was still here. Alone.

He'd done a fair amount of drinking in the last two years. But it didn't solve his problems. Hell, these days it didn't even stop the pain or give him some oblivion.

It gave him a migraine-quality hangover. Hell getting older. More to forget, and he couldn't even drink the memories gone.

Elijah sat at the table and watched the two younger men work their way to the bar. He hid a grin. Rafe was trying hard not to look at the dancers. Joe Bob, though, was a natural for a place like this. By the time he had a beer in hand, he also had six new friends. He didn't even look back at Elijah but joined his new friends at their table right in front.

Rafe sat down at the table with his back to the dancers and handed Elijah a beer. "I so don't belong here," he said with a sigh.

Elijah laughed. "First time in a stripper bar?"

Rafe nodded. "And last."

Elijah laughed again. "You're supposed to have a reputation with the ladies."

Rafe shook his head. "Maybe so. But that has nothing to do with this. This is...," he shrugged helplessly, at loss for words.

"Wish I'd been as smart as you when I was your age," Elijah muttered.

"I don't get it," Rafe admitted.

Elijah considered the crowd. "You've got a couple of groups here," he said. "Mostly young sailors who may or may not have a girl in town. They come to drink with their buddies and to remind themselves what a girl looks like. The married ones? I don't get them either, although a few have their wives with them here, and I really don't get them."

"If I had a wife, I wouldn't bring her here," Rafe said vehemently. "And I wouldn't be here either, I'd be home with her."

Elijah swallowed a lump in his throat and blinked a couple of times. He-man pilots don't cry in titty bars, he reminded himself. "Yeah."

Rafe looked appalled. "I'm sorry, I didn't mean...," he trailed off.

Elijah took a long pull on the beer and waved off his comment.

"Then you got the old sourdoughs," he said. "They aren't going to ever see a woman — much less a young female body like these — in their beds again. They come, drink, enjoy them, then go home and jerk off. A few of the girls might sell themselves out the back door, but probably not. Those women are found elsewhere."

"That's gross," Rafe protested.

"Let it be a lesson to you, kid. Grab yourself a good woman while you're young enough to attract one. Hold on for all you're worth. Up here? Women have the upper hand. Not enough to go around. They can be choosy. And they should be."

"You talk like you're an old man," Rafe said. "You're not that much older than I am."

"29. And it's not the years, it's the miles," Elijah said. "You're what? 24?"

Rafe nodded. "Good guess."

"Nah, I used to help Lanky with his paperwork before Dace showed up. Whenever he was between office managers. God help us both."

Rafe laughed. Lanky had been notorious for chasing away office managers. Until Dace, three months had been the record. The shortest time? The guy hadn't come back from lunch.

Rafe looked around the room, spotting the groups that Elijah had identified. "And that table?" he said, gesturing with his head. "They don't fit in either group."

Elijah followed his gesture. "Well, now," he said slowly. "Things might just be more interesting tonight than I thought. That's Ben Daniels, the owner of the bar, and one of the most powerful men in Sitka."

"How do you know him?"

"I used to fly in and out of Sitka regularly when I was your age," he replied, not taking his eyes off Daniels' table. "Paid to know who had power in a town."

"You know the others?"

"Yeah. One is Swede Johansen, runs the fish packing plant in town."

"And the third man?"

"That's what makes it so interesting," Elijah said slowly. "That's Duke Campbell. Police chief Duke Campbell."

Rafe looked at Elijah and then looked at Joe Bob down by the stage. "We ought to get out of here," he said.

Joe Bob liked people. All kinds of people. But he especially liked guys who knew how to party. And these sailors — don't call them Coasties out loud, he reminded himself — could hold their own with the best. He was older than them, but not by much, Coast Guard sailors stayed in for a while. And he was only 28.

One of them was telling a story about their ship. Gotta love a sailor. They had a girl in every port, but when they talked with that gleam in their eye, they were talking about their ship.

The ship in the story was the Clover. And apparently, some guys hung over the side and painted out the C, before they pulled into port one night. The guys thought this was hilarious, even though it meant extra duty and they had to spend personal time repainting the whole name because the paint wouldn't match.

Joe Bob laughed too. It was funny. Something the guys on the Slope would have done. Men with time on their hands found pranks to do, which is why the bosses — be they boatswain's mates in the Coast Guard, or crew boss on the Slope — kept them busy.

Someone told about a guy who was back on flight duty for the first time after he crashed a copter on the other side of the island. Even two months later everyone was still in awe that he'd survived it.

"So, he shows up for equipment check," said a crewman, gesturing with his beer and laughing at his own story. "And he has us walk through the check three times! Three times! He says he used up all his luck last time out, and from here on, he needed to be extra cautious."

"Did you do the check?" Joe Bob asked.

"Hell yes, we did. Did a fourth time too. I mean, he's right. He used up the luck."

The men around the table nodded solemnly.

Joe Bob laughed. "I heard someone went out chasing mountain goats again."

They all groaned. "We're cleaning below decks for that one," one man grumbled. "Bunch of fools."

"OK grandpa," one of the younger men said good-naturedly. "You tell me you never did that your first enlistment up here."

He laughed. "Smart enough not to get caught. We did it on scheduled surveillance trips. Who's fool enough to take a copter out unauthorized?"

Some grunts of agreement.

"Unauthorized? Surprised they didn't get court martialed," Joe Bob said to keep the story going. He was surprised though.

"Pays to know people," the talkative young guy said. "I guess when you're buds with the police chief's son-in-law, they don't throw the book at you."

"No, we'll all be on the floor of the ship with toothbrushes for the week," someone said sourly.

"Takes balls, though. No brains. But balls," Joe Bob said cheerfully. "What's his name? He deserves a toast."

"To Marc DuChamp and his merry band," someone said, raising his beer.

"To Marc," everyone echoed.

Someone grabbed his arm, and Joe Bob looked up to see Rafe. "We need to leave," Rafe said in a low voice.

"We just got here," Joe Bob protested.

"JB, we need to leave *now*. Elijah," he hesitated, and then brightened, "Elijah's sick. Unless you want to clean up vomit in the back of the bar, we need to go."

"Shit," Joe Bob said. "Sorry, guys. We got a lightweight drinker, I guess. And I'm not going to clean up after him here."

The guys laughed. Joe Bob got up, tossed some money on the table. He took a look at the dancers' and shook his head. Damn it, he didn't get a chance to confirm the story about them being Coast Guard wives.

Rafe was moving fast toward the back door. Joe Bob frowned. Then Elijah was at his back.

"Look back toward your buddies, and then do a sweep to your right," Elijah said softly.

Joe Bob did and kept moving.

"See the oddball table?"

"Yeah."

"One of them is Duke Campbell. He's with Ben Daniels and Swede Johansen."

Joe Bob moved just a bit faster. "Hang in there, man," he said, grabbing Elijah's arm. "Fresh air will do you good."

"Wh...," Elijah said puzzled. Then shut up as they reached the bouncer. He opened the door for them, and they were outside. Rafe was waiting for them on the deck.

"OK, so that doesn't look good," Joe Bob admitted. "Who was the woman?"

"Woman?" Elijah asked as he unlocked the car.

"Some woman came out of the bathrooms and joined them as we were leaving. Heavy set woman but dressed meticulously," Joe Bob stumbled a bit over the word. Shit, he'd had more to drink than he thought. "In her 50s? Didn't belong there, that's for sure."

"No idea," Elijah said, as he pulled out of the parking lot. "One of their wives."

Rafe shook his head. "No way. Those men wouldn't bring their wives out to that bar."

Elijah conceded that point. "Sorry you didn't have time to get a name," he said.

"You underestimate me," Joe Bob said smugly. "Marc DuChamp and friends."

"Well, damn," Elijah said. "Back to the hotel? Or Dr. Kitka's place?"

Joe Bob pulled out his phone and punched in a number. "Captain, I've got a name."

Rafe looked back toward the bar. It was dark enough that it was hard to see who was standing on the deck looking after them. It could be the bouncer, but he didn't think so. Whoever it was had their phone out and was talking to someone. He pocketed the phone and turned back into the bar.

"Guys, I think we need to park this car and walk back along the beach," he said slowly.

Elijah looked in the rearview mirror at the bar. "You see something?"

"Yeah. Maybe being paranoid, but," he trailed off and shrugged.

Elijah pulled off into the parking lot of an apartment complex, parking in a visitor's space. He didn't want some tribal member's car to get towed.

"Better call your boss back," Elijah said. "He can give Mr. Kitka a heads up about the car."

Joe Bob nodded, and talking softly, he told the captain what was up.

"He says he can send a car after us," Joe Bob said, looking up.

Elijah smiled. "I think it will be interesting to walk along the beach. See if a cop car comes out this way. Or if there's a checkpoint set up on the way back. We'll be able to see from the beach."

"OK," Joe Bob said. He looked at the cowboy boots he had on and shrugged.

Ten minutes later, a cop car headed toward the bar from town. The men looked at each other and grinned.

After ten minutes the car slowly headed back into town, its prowl lights doing sweeps of the sidewalks and the beach.

Rafe sat down on a large rock at the edge between beach and dunes. The other men looked at him, quizzically. "Movement is easy to track. A group is harder to see if they're sitting down. Harder to count," he explained.

"Do I want to know how you know that?" Joe Bob drawled, as he sat down on the sand next to him.

"Trust me, a Hispanic boy like me in Anchorage learns how to look inconspicuous," Rafe said.

"Hard to picture you running from the cops," Elijah said, as he perched next to him. He twisted so he could see the road. Another cop car crawled by.

"Not the cops. Other kids."

"Joe Bob, I think you better call the captain. Have him come get us. Maybe in Elizabeth Kitka's car."

Joe Bob nodded and made the call.

The captain pulled up to the pullout, and the three men piled in quickly. Wyckoff pulled away smoothly.

"Maybe we're being paranoid," Joe Bob said apologetically.

"Apparently not," Wyckoff said, as flashing lights went on behind him. He pulled over, pulled out his state patrol identification as well as his driver's license.

He rolled down the window. "Something wrong, officer?" he said coldly.

"Who are you?" the officer said startled. "That's Kitka's car."

"Yes, it is Dr. Kitka's car," Wyckoff said with an emphasis on Dr. "If you look at my identification, you can see who I am."

"Why don't you all get out of the car?" the officer said.

"Look at the ID," Wyckoff said calmly, making no move to get out.

"I said," the officer began, and then looked down at the identification in his hand and swallowed. "Captain Wyckoff. I didn't recognize you."

"Undoubtedly. But I would expect more courtesy from any officer toward anyone. Why did you pull me over?"

"Uh, we had a report of a suspicious group of men casing the area," he stammered.

"And you thought they might be driving Dr. Kitka's car?"

"No, sir," he said, sounding terribly young. "I made a mistake."

"Name and badge number?" Wyckoff asked. "We can discuss this with your boss tomorrow. Among other things."

The officer stammered through that information. Joe Bob found a small notebook in the glovebox and wrote it down.

"And my ID back," Wyckoff said, holding out his hand.

The officer swallowed visibly as he handed the identification back.

"Drive safely, sir," he said. His voice squeaked a bit.

Wyckoff nodded once. Rolled up his window and drove back into town.

"Man, I kinda feel sorry for him," Joe Bob said.

"Been the recipient of that kind of dressing down, have you?" Elijah said with a laugh from the back seat.

"Yeah," he said with feeling.

Wyckoff permitted himself a small half-smile. "So, I counted three patrol cars out on this road," he said. "Why?"

Joe Bob shook his head. "I don't really know. Something made Duke curious, or suspicious, of us. But he knows we're in town, so the idea we'd be out drinking? Not a big surprise."

"Maybe not at a strip club," Wyckoff said.

"Maybe not," he conceded. "But then, in Sitka?"

"I think it was the woman," Rafe said.

"A woman?" Wyckoff glanced at the young pilot in his rearview mirror.

"There was the chief, Daniels, and Swede," Elijah said. "I recognized them. As we were leaving, Joe Bob said a woman came out from the bathroom and joined them. I didn't see her."

"Describe her," Wyckoff said.

Joe Bob paused to picture her in his mind. "Maybe in her 50s. You know how some heavy older women dress carefully to hide their weight, but kind of flamboyant? She was like that. Hair was perfect. Clothes. Jewelry. I couldn't see details, couldn't see her features. She carried herself well."

"She didn't belong," Rafe said. "The whole table was wrong, but if one of them owned the bar, no one would be too surprised. But she's not the kind of woman to watch a stripper."

"Which makes it the perfect place for her to meet with those men and not be seen by anyone she knows," Wyckoff said softly.

"In Sitka?" Elijah said. "Why not in someone's home? A bar is risky."

Wyckoff shrugged as he used his signals before turning onto Elizabeth Kitka's street. "Three married men meeting at some woman's house? Neighbors notice. A cafe? You bump into her friends."

"I wish I could describe her better," Joe Bob said. "I bet Elizabeth Kitka knows her."

"Yes," Wyckoff said. "I bet she does, too."

Chapter 17

(Sitka. 3 1/2 Mile Club. Tuesday night.)
"I don't know what was so important we needed to actually get together," she groused as she returned from the ladies' room.

Maybe the ladies' room was in better shape than the men's room at the 3 1/2 Mile Club, Ben Daniels thought, because he wouldn't use the men's room no matter how urgent it got.

This had been his first bar. Seedy. A stripper bar. He had struck pay dirt when he found that bored Coast Guard wives would strip while their husbands were out to sea. Thirty years on, God, 40 years, he still didn't get that dynamic. But it had been profitable for him. And it didn't seem to increase the divorce rate, so what the hell.

The crowd tonight was the usual mix of old sourdoughs, rowdy sailors, and a few tourists from out of town. He could always spot the tourists.

"You see those three tourists?" Swede said as the men in question were leaving. Hadn't been there long.

"Yeah," Ben said.

"Pretty sure one of them is Elijah Calhoun. He used to fly in here pretty regularly back in the day. Before that accident."

The entire state of Alaska was a small gossipy town, Ben thought, torn between being appalled and amused.

Duke was drinking steadily. "So?"

"He used to fly for Lanky Purdue," Swede said levelly.

Duke stared at him until it clicked. "You think he's spying on us for Lanky?"

"Don't know how he'd even think we'd be here," Swede said. "But he saw us."

Duke was up and out the door before Ben could stop him.

"He's going to get us all locked up," the woman complained. "Why did he want us to meet anyway?"

"So, he can say we were all in on it," Ben said sourly. "Whatever it is he's done now."

Swede shook his head. "I owe him, but not this much. I'm gone." He stood up. So did the woman.

"I'm leaving too," she announced. "I can't afford to be linked to this, Ben. I can't."

Ben nodded. He understood. None of them could, but here they were. Sucked into Duke's vortex. And Duke was spinning out of control.

Duke came back in. "Called my boys," he said with satisfaction. "They'll get a sweep going. We'll find out what Calhoun is up to and who those other men were."

"What difference does it make, Duke?" Ben demanded. "You need to shut this down."

Duke slammed his empty beer glass down. "That's what I'm doing," he said. "Toss those three in jail if I have to. Run Wyckoff out of my town. What does he think he's doing, coming into my town, asking questions, setting up a command center in my office!"

"Quiet down," Ben said, as Duke's voice got louder. "You want this whole bar to hear you?"

"Where did the other two go?" Duke said, his voice back in a normal range. "Did you hear me? Wyckoff is running an investigation into what he calls 'the disappearance of one of my officers.' He's asking questions. Not just about the Kitka boys and that girl. But about Luke Kitka and other...," he fumbled, looking for the right word. "What did he call them? Questionable incidents. Who does he think he is?"

"A captain in the Alaska State Patrol, apparently," Ben said dryly. "Does he have the authority to do this? He's out of his territory. Surely you have some connections in Juneau who can rein him in."

Duke nodded morosely. His mood swing from explosive anger to depression worried Ben.

"Yeah, I called in a few favors. But they're all hands-off on this one. A patrol officer is missing, one guy said. You need to help Wyckoff find him and then he'll be out of your hair."

Ben snorted. "I guess you could try that."

Duke slumped back in his chair. "I was hoping Swede might try his connections." He looked at the empty chairs. "Or hers. But I guess not."

"Neither of them want to get involved in Kitka's disappearance," Ben told him. "And neither do I. Tell me straight, Duke, is there any chance he's still alive and you can stage a rescue? Blame Mike for it? Look like a hero?"

Duke brightened at the idea, but then shook his head. "My daughter loves the bastard," he said. "I can't throw him to the wolves."

"Duke you've got to do something. Wyckoff is not going away willingly. And it sounds like he's got enough sway in the capital to stop you from forcing him out of here. What are you going to do?"

Duke stood up. He looked around the bar, and then headed back out the door. "I'll figure out something," he said. "This is my town. And I aim to keep it that way."

Ben watched him go. He sighed and shook his head. Then carrying his glass of scotch — which came from a special bottle the bartender kept for him — he walked through the crowd, mingling, talking, until he came to the table of sailors the one tourist had been at.

"You all toasting someone," he asked congenially.

"Yeah, lifting a glass to the bozo who took a helicopter out unauthorized and got us all cleaning the decks with toothbrushes," one happy drunk said. "Here's to Marc DuChamp, leader of the merry band."

Ben smiled, but it didn't go to his eyes. "I can drink to that," he said. "Let me buy a round."

So, whoever that was, they had the name of the pilot Mike used, Ben thought as they young men cheered his offer of a free drink. Wyckoff was circling closer.

Ben had started carrying a weapon these last few days. He hadn't done that in more than a decade. But these felt like old times. And in the old days, he never left the house without being armed. He wasn't sure what good a gun was going to do. This wasn't the kind of trouble a gun could get you out of. Still, it felt better to have it.

He patted the shoulder of one of the sailors and moved on to another table. Just being a good bar owner. Glad-handing the customers. Nothing to see here, folks, just a barkeep having a drink with the police chief and a couple of old friends.

In a titty bar. Ben shook his head. It had been Duke's idea. And truthfully, it wasn't a bad one. No one from any of their circles would see them out here. But right now? He didn't want to be seen with the police chief at all. Not by anyone.

And wasn't that a hell of a thing?

Chapter 18

(Sitka. Mt. Edgecombe Coast Guard station. Wednesday.)

It was early when Wyckoff roused the Coast Guard commander out of bed. He explained very succinctly what he needed. Or rather who.

"You'll have them," the commander said. "They've been on deck duty ever since they got back. But that's when I thought it was just hijinks."

Wyckoff took Lanky with him. Lanky seemed to think he was his guard dog, Wyckoff thought with amusement. But he was grateful for the man's company. And he didn't doubt the old man could hold his own in a fight if necessary. Not that it should be necessary at the Coast Guard base, but as screwed up as this whole investigation was, who knew?

The base still looked like Army surplus Wyckoff noted. Metal buildings, mostly hangars and repair shops, and one building of offices. That's where they headed.

The commander himself greeted the two men.

"They're waiting for you," he said sourly. "I didn't tell them a thing."

Wyckoff was unprepared for how young they looked. Mid-20s, probably. When did that start looking so young? He wondered. It made him a bit grouchy.

"Attention!" the boatswain's mate in the room called when the commander walked back in. The sailors straightened, eyes forward.

Wyckoff walked in front of them. He'd worn his uniform for the occasion. And he saw one of them mouth "oh shit" at the sight.

"All right, two nights ago, you gentlemen took a helicopter out unauthorized, dropped three people out somewhere in the wilderness, and left them to die," he said coldly. "Why?"

He looked them over. "Which one of you is Marc DuChamp?"

"Sir," one of them said, startled.

"Explain."

The tall young man swallowed. "Yes, sir. Uh. I received a call from the assistant police chief requesting our assistance." He stopped, looked at the base commander and then at the state patrol captain in front of him. He swallowed again. "He said he had knowledge that there was going to be an attempted jail break of a man who had killed a police officer. And that the killer was too well-connected to ever stand trial. He wanted our assistance in...," he paused, swallowed again, and blurted the rest out, "what he termed frontier-style justice."

The base commander made a sound that was a cross between a moan and fury, but he said nothing.

"I see," Wyckoff said. "And what did this justice consist of?"

"We were at the jail conducting surveillance, when sure enough, a young woman approached the jail and returned with the suspected killer. We intervened and took all three people into custody."

Wyckoff could see the base commander out of the corner of his eye. He hoped the man didn't have a heart attack.

"So, you believed that the young woman was able to overcome the jailor and release the suspect?" Wyckoff asked. The men stared at him startled. Apparently thinking through the logistics of this hadn't occurred to them. "Never mind. Give my companion the coordinates."

When he hesitated, Wyckoff barked, "*Now!*"

One of the other young men pulled a notebook from his pocket and rattled off longitude and latitude.

Lanky Purdue nodded. "On it," he said, and ducked out the door.

"OK, you were telling me why you thought this was a legitimate operation of the Sitka Police Department," Wyckoff said, his tone dry. "Well?"

"We know Mike Anderson, sir," Duchamp said, barely above a whisper. "He was one of us. So, we did what he asked."

"Did you ask who they were?"

"One of them, the one who stayed with the car, said he was a lieutenant in the Alaska state patrol, but that was obviously a lie." He trailed off, looking at Wyckoff's uniform. "Shit."

"Why did you think that was a lie, sailor?" Wyckoff asked him.

"He was an Alaskan Native," another young man volunteered when it was obvious that DuChamp wasn't going to. "Never seen a Native cop around here."

"I see," Wyckoff said. His fury threatened to rise up and choke him before he got through this.

"And the girl? That didn't seem strange to you?"

Another man spoke up. "That bothered me. I slipped her my knife and made sure her ropes were cut before we left them. That wasn't right."

Wyckoff saw the base commander close his eyes. The tragedy was these weren't bad men. Young. Stupid. So very stupid. Easily led. And their careers were over. They'd be lucky not to serve time.

"So, you dumped three people in a remote area in Southeast Alaska, tied in ropes, and generously gave them a knife."

DuChamp swallowed. "Yes, sir," he whispered. "Mike said it would teach them a lesson. That he'd collect them and haul them back for trial."

"For your information, one of those men was indeed my officer. His brother, a Fish and Game warden. And the woman was a pilot who flies for the man who just left here. I suggest you avoid him at all costs, because he would kill you all right now and not give it a second thought." And he'd help him, Wyckoff thought grimly. The chances of finding them alive was small. Very small.

"What was your officer doing breaking a man out of jail?" one of the men asked indignantly.

"Shut up, Jim," DuChamp said. "We were misled, sir," he said to Wyckoff.

"Misled?" the commander roared. "Misled? I don't think you realize what trouble you're in. You face court martial. You will probably face criminal charges of kidnapping. Your lives are effectively over."

Wyckoff felt like he was re-enacting a scene from *A Few Good Men*. As restaged by Gomer Pyle. He felt sick. And he'd have his justice when Assistant Police Chief Mike Anderson was in jail for the rest of his life. Not just for the deaths of Paul and the others, but for the destruction of these men's lives as well. People he called friends, apparently. Duke still knew how to spot a sociopath and turn him to his advantage.

"You'd better pray they're found alive, or I'll have you up on murder charges," Wyckoff said.

The men looked at each other. The one who had given Dace his knife looked sick. Wyckoff didn't feel sorry for him. He'd known what they were doing was wrong. But they'd come back to base, and he hadn't said a word.

"Why didn't you say something when you got back?" Wyckoff asked him.

He shook his head. "Mike. Mike was our buddy," he said. "I figured it had to be OK. He wouldn't...," he trailed off.

"Wouldn't set you up to take the fall for murder?" Wyckoff asked softly. He looked at the commander.

"I'll need copies of your interrogation," he said. "It's time to clean house at the Sitka Police Department."

Wyckoff's driver was still waiting outside. "Lanky?" he asked.

The man, Bobby Kitka, nodded toward the airport. "I took him down there, came back for you. He was calling in his pilot," he said. "But he didn't sound happy. Not good news?"

Wyckoff hesitated. "How are you related to Paul and Jonas?" he asked.

The driver started the car. "That bad, aye?" he said, using a British Columbia slang. Southeast Alaskan Tlingits had more relatives in BC than they did in Alaska. "I'm their uncle. Luke Jr., was my older brother."

"It's not good," Wyckoff admitted. "They dumped them bound and helpless out in the Tongass. Left them a knife, because one felt sorry for the girl. We've got the coordinates but who knows what we'll find. Bodies, I'm afraid. God damn it."

Bobby Kitka shook his head. "I doubt it. Jonas armed with a knife? Paul may have gotten soft working for you all," he said, with a teasing side look, "but Jonas hasn't forgotten his upbringing. I helped train him. He'll be alive. And he'll keep the other two alive as well."

Wyckoff felt better. "Let's go talk to the police chief."

"I can tell you one thing," Bobby added as he drove back across the bridge to Sitka. "Those guys who dumped three people in the Tongass had better stay on base. They're dead men in this town. And no jury will convict. White, brown, makes no difference. The land here is unforgiving, and you just don't set up anyone for that kind of risk. Not even your worst enemy."

Wyckoff closed his eyes. He didn't think the commander was planning on letting those men out of the brig — did they have a brig? — but he'd talk to him just in case. "They thought the assistant police chief had authorized it."

Bobby Kitka snorted. "Mike Anderson? Yeah, I just bet he did. That man is bone crazy. Duke found himself a kindred spirit and took him home to meet his daughter. Maybe Duke can keep him in line for his daughter's sake. Or maybe...," he trailed off. "Or maybe she was looking for a man like her father."

Ripples, Wyckoff thought. He came here to find his officer. Now he had a police department to clean up. A Coast Guard base in turmoil, with some sailors up on charges, and a psychopath. Two psychopaths to tend with.

Unlike Lanky, who had shadowed him yesterday when Wyckoff went into the police station, Bobby Kitka had just laughed. "Nope," he said. "I won't do you any good, not in there. You put my number on speed dial, and your finger on the dial button, and I'll send in the Indians to rescue you from the cavalry."

He laughed at his joke. It even made Wyckoff chuckle. "You do that," he said.

The dispatcher wasn't making any jokes this morning. She was a woman from the Bronx approaching retirement — and Wyckoff bet that was a story worth hearing — who sounded like she was a chain smoker in her off hours.

"Chief in?" Wyckoff asked, heading toward the back.

She nodded, picked up the phone and let Duke know he had a visitor.

Duke came around his desk and stuck out his hand. "Been awhile, Andrew," he said. Wyckoff shook his hand.

"Yes, it has," he said. "What progress have you made in locating my officer?"

Duke Campbell went back around his desk and sat down. "My assistant chief Mike Anderson is leading the manhunt for both Kitkas," he said. "We have a BOLO out for their arrests."

Wyckoff grew still. "On what charges?"

"What charges? Jonas was charged with murder, remember? Now he's got breaking out of jail to go with it, and assault on my jailor. And your 'officer' is charged with aiding and abetting."

"Cut the shit, Duke," Wyckoff said. "The jail called Dr. Kitka's house and told her Jonas was being released. Seth Jones was there and heard the whole thing. Paul and the pilot who flew him here, Candace Marshall, went to pick Jonas up. They were kidnapped and dumped in the Tongass on the orders of your assistant chief."

"You don't know that!" Duke stood up, put his hands on his desk and roared back at Wyckoff. "You're making shit up to cover for your officer!"

Wyckoff shook his head. "You stupid f-ck," he said in a low enough voice so that Duke's officers wouldn't overhear. "If you planned this, you did a piss poor job, because it's got holes all through it. And if you didn't plan it, you've got an assistant chief staging a coup and planning to take you down. Either way? You're done here."

"This is my town, Wyckoff," Duke Campbell hissed at him. "You don't come into my town and make threats. I'll throw you in jail, too. See if I won't."

Wyckoff laughed at him. "You can try. You tried to get me pulled from town already, didn't you? How did that go? I'm still here. Now where is this Anderson? I want a progress report on his 'manhunt.'"

Duke sat down, leaned back in his chair. "He's out hunting, Wyckoff," he said with a half-smile. "He's out hunting."

Wyckoff stopped cold. The two men locked stares.

"Listen to me, now, Campbell," Wyckoff said. "I will hold you personally responsible for the well-being of my officer and his companions. Do you hear me? You. No matter who looks to be at fault. No matter what the details are or the facts you try to present to the state inquiry board when it's convened.

"No don't interrupt me," Wyckoff said, in a deadly quiet voice. "There will be a state inquiry board, and I will have your badge for the mismanagement I'm seeing here. And you'd better pray that Paul Kitka is present to testify at the inquiry, or I will have you up on murder charges. And there's a whole lot of men at the state pen who would be eager to see you."

Duke leaped to his feet, but Wyckoff didn't flinch. "Get out," Campbell shouted. "Get out of my office. I run the tightest ship in the state. Have you ever looked at our serious crime stats? We're so god damn low people can't believe them. I take care of this city. Good care — and have for nearly 40 years. No one comes in here and threatens me. Especially not some state patrol pussy like you. Get out."

"Oh, I'm going," Wyckoff said. "You've got some calls to make. Find that man of yours, Campbell. And find mine."

Three grim-faced officers were standing in the main office when Wyckoff walked out. Bobby Kitka was standing at the window bullshitting with the dispatcher, who was laughing while keeping a wary eye on the officers arrayed behind her.

Bobby looked up. "Good," he said. "I was just going to have her interrupt you two. Lanky radioed the tower with a message. They found the landing site, found where they'd been. But they're gone. They're going to do flyovers and see if they can spot them, but they're not hopeful they'll be spotted in that old growth forest. Probably won't be able to see them until they reach the beach."

Wyckoff closed his eyes in relief. "That's good news."

"Yeah. But you know what's odd? It's the same tiny island where Hank Petras disappeared last week. Weird, huh?" Bobby Kitka said. His eyes were cold, and he held himself as if he were prepared to be jumped.

Wyckoff marched through the officers, and they parted for him. He didn't even pause. "That is weird," Wyckoff said. He turned back toward the officers, "Don't you think that's weird? That Anderson would have his Coast Guard buddies kidnap folks and dump them in the same place where he took out an orienteering group and got one of his officers killed? Don't you think that's strange?"

He looked at each one, memorizing their faces. One was the young officer who had stopped them last night on the road home from the bar. "Any of you on that orienteering trip?"

No one said a word.

"You guys sure got those lab results back fast on that blood sample," he added conversationally. "You all got an in with the state labs? Why, it can take us weeks to get results back."

Silence.

Wyckoff nodded. "If anyone has information you'd like to share, dispatch has my phone number."

He walked out side by side with Bobby Kitka.

"Man, I don't know if you've got the biggest balls I've seen — and I did two tours in Kuwait — or if you're just crazy," Bobby said in a low voice as he unlocked the car.

"He had the goddamn audacity to brag about how low his serious crime stats are!" Wyckoff fumed.

Bobby Kitka started laughing, the bent-over, laughing-until-tears-came kind of laugh. Wyckoff stared at him.

"Oh my God, he didn't," he said. "He throws that in everyone's faces. And they back down, because shit? He must be doing something right, yes? Do you know why he has such low stats for serious crime? Because there has never been a felony car theft in this city probably since the first car arrived. I mean where are they going to go with it?"

Wyckoff started laughing.

"So, you have Anchorage with the second highest auto theft rate in the god-damn country, and you have Sitka with none? Of course his stats look good! You know what you get charged with here? Misdemeanor joy riding — usually kids or a drunk. Was a rash of them when Toyota only made a few keys and people would come out of the bar, get in a car, and drive off — in the wrong car. Remember that? Here, it's the owner who is likely to get charged — with leaving the key in the car. I can't believe he pulled that shit on you!"

Wyckoff snorted. "And now everyone in there, including Duke, just got a look at us out here laughing like hyenas, and thinking we're laughing about them?"

Bobby Kitka grinned at him. He got in the car.

"And you did that deliberately, too," Bobby said.

Wyckoff walked around the car and got in the passenger seat. He studied the man and grinned. "OK, increase their paranoia and who knows? Maybe someone will talk."

Then he sighed. "If you've served, you know what you're seeing then," he said. He sat for a moment, his head tipped back against the head rest, his eyes closed.

Bobby didn't start the car. "Pack behavior. Us against them. They see themselves as an exclusive team and everyone is their enemy. They pride themselves on taking care of their own, but their own isn't this town, or the people who live here, it's them. The blue brotherhood."

Wyckoff nodded. "And it's not even uncommon in police forces for that to develop. If you have a good leader, they can stop it. But Duke Campbell has been encouraging it. He's been building it in, for decades.

"He hires men from out of town — fresh out of academy. They get here, they're young, they've got families, some of them, and they probably can't afford to leave even if they wanted to. The older cops help the new ones settle in. There's an apartment in the same complex as some others live. Here's a good daycare center for your children, run by the lieutenant's wife. We're having some people in Friday, help you get acquainted. All officers and their families, you'll like them," Wyckoff paused.

"They never get to know the community," Bobby acknowledged. "Some have tried, Dad said, but they don't last long."

"No, I don't suppose they do. Either Campbell ran them out, or they could see what kind of a department it was and got out as soon as they could afford to," Wyckoff said. "So, isolation. And then, cultural norms. You protect your fellow officers. So what if he roughed up a drunk? Well the drunk swung at him, you saw it, didn't you? Didn't you? Then at some point you cross into a gray zone yourself, and someone covers for you, and you're grateful."

Wyckoff shook his head. "I heard a police reform consultant talk once. A former cop, a Black guy out of Baltimore."

"Rough city," Bobby observed.

"Yeah. He said something that stuck with me. He said 20 percent of the cops in any department are good cops. They'll do what's right, no matter the pressure, no matter the cop culture. And 20 percent are bad apples. The other 60 percent will follow the leader. If the chief is a good leader, then you'll have good cops, a good department. If he's a shitty leader? You get bad cops.

"Reform is simple, he said," Wyckoff continued. He was beginning to come down off the adrenaline rush of the confrontation. "You hire good police chiefs. You get rid of the bad apples, and you don't let anyone else hire them. That's it. That's what you have to do."

"And if you have a narcissistic megalomaniac personality that is spiraling out of control?" Bobby asked as he started up his car.

Wyckoff stared at him. "What exactly is it that you do when you're not chauffeuring people for your father?"

Bobby Kitka laughed but didn't answer. "Well, am I wrong about him?"

Wyckoff shook his head. "No, I think that's exactly what's going on. The problem with a psychopath like that is they have such a tight grasp of their view of reality that they suck others into it. You lay out an argument, and they nod and agree. And then they reiterate how they see it, and you realize they didn't hear a word. Then you give up and go along, because what's the use in fighting it? And the next thing you know, you've destroyed your career like those Coast Guard sailors have for Mike Anderson."

"That may be what the flashpoint is," said Dr. Robert "Bobby" Kitka, psychologist at the Native Health Clinic – and sometime chauffeur for his father. "He saw Mike Anderson as his protégé. But Anderson has the same ideation as Campbell. And he's younger. Hungrier. He marries the boss's daughter. He's moving in for the kill. Campbell can't face it. He knows someone is coming for him, but he can't believe it's a man he treats like a son. So, he attacks Petras. Then Jonas. The threat is real, it's the source he can't see."

Wyckoff nodded thoughtfully. "Yes, exactly like that."

"So, what are you going to do about it?" Kitka said with challenge in his voice.

"I'm going to see it dismantled, brick by brick, cop by cop," Wyckoff said. "Get rid of the bad apples — and at this point they are all bad apples — and find a good man for Sitka to hire as a chief."

"Then let's go get Lanky Purdue," Bobby Kitka said, and headed back out to the airport. "Or he might start that dismantling project all by himself."

Lanky looked old and tired when they picked him up by the dock where his float plane was tethered.

"I thought it would be a safe, easy trip for her to solo on," he said. "I thought her worst problem would be this airport, because it's got a rep for being tricky, especially if there is any weather to speak of. So, I focused on weather reports, and didn't think about Kitka going home. Damn me."

"You knew about Paul's past here?" Wyckoff asked. He was having some of the same kind of moments.

"Remembered there was a past. You know how Alaska is. One small town spread across nearly 700,000 square miles. Been 20 years, though. Didn't remember the details. But a Native Alaskan in trouble in Sitka — should have been enough. She wouldn't have come here if I hadn't said it was OK."

"Someone would have to have brought Paul down to Sitka," Wyckoff said.

"Could have been me," Lanky said morosely.

"Oh, stop with the blame," Bobby said disgustedly. "Neither of you are at fault. Blame goes where it needs to: Duke Campbell and Mike Anderson. Focus, people!"

Lanky stared at him, then looked at Wyckoff, who just shrugged. "You heard the man."

Chapter 19

(The Tongass. Wednesday, early.)

When Dace woke up she was snuggled against Paul's chest. It was just the two of them; she didn't know where Jonas had gone. She could hear Paul's heart beating. She smiled, relaxed, contented to listen to the steady sound. She was pretty sure Paul was still asleep.

It gave her courage to touch — well maybe not courage, that was too strong a term — but she smoothed her hand across the muscles of his chest. Even through his shirt, she could feel the hard muscles of his pecs. He was firm and youthful — Dace stopped that thought. She didn't need to compare him to her husband. That was in the past; this was now.

Paul was not a big man, just under six feet tall, and that much height was because of his mother. His Tlingit relatives were shorter than he was, although not as short as the Inuit in the Denali region and outward. He was slim, but he worked out to develop muscle strength. Breaking up bar fights was hard work, he'd told her once, and it took strength. Or brains, and since there wasn't much he could do about that, he worked on the muscles. She smiled at the memory.

She moved her hand lower to his abs. She wanted to knead them, to clench her fist in them, but she knew that would waken Paul, and she wasn't brave enough to start something when he was awake. But it had been so long since she'd been held and could believe it meant something to the man who held her. She felt so hungry for touch. For the feeling of a man's body against hers, for the heat they radiated. Why was it that men seemed to put off so much more heat? It wasn't as if she had tons of experience. A couple of boyfriends and then there had been Stephen Whitaker, the man she'd married. He'd been a good lover, she admitted, but when he started.... She shut down that thought too.

Better to enjoy the feel of this man, in the here and now, while he was sleeping, and she could.

Except he was awake. "Are you going to move your hand any lower?" he said, in a sexy rumble. "Because if you are, I'm not going to be able to hold still and pretend to be asleep any longer."

Dace snatched her hand away from his chest and buried her face in the crook of his arm. She knew she was blazing red.

Paul took her hand back and placed it back where it had been on his abs. "I like having you touch me, Dace," he said quietly. "I just didn't know if you were ready for this."

Dace held very still. Then she looked up at him, and with a trembling smile, she pressed her lips against his. Startled, he didn't react for a moment, and then he took over the kiss, nibbling at her mouth, tasting her lips, waiting for her to open herself to him.

She opened her mouth, letting his tongue seek hers, deepening the kiss.

"Sorry to interrupt, guys," Jonas said. His voice coming from just a few feet away made Dace jump. Her face turned red, again, and she hid her face against Paul's shoulder. Paul was pleased — she'd turned to him; she hadn't pulled away. He tightened his arms in a reassuring hug.

"We do need to get a move on, however," Jonas continued. "We don't know how far we've got to go until we find water. And I think it's going to rain."

By the time they started in single file down the trail Paul had spotted the day before, it was raining. Dace tipped her face up and tried to catch some of the raindrops. She laughed as the drops fell into her eyes more than into her mouth.

"Thirsty?" Paul asked, smiling as he watched her. It had been a long time since they'd had water. They were all feeling it. If it weren't for the mild weather and the water-saturated air, they'd be in trouble already. Still, they needed to find water soon. Or figure a way to capture the rain.

Dace tried for another drop, hamming it up, not wanting to whine about her thirst. She stumbled over a root. "Right," she said. "I best watch where I'm going."

Paul laughed.

"So, this is the Tongass," Dace said, walking slower so she could talk. If she couldn't talk, she was walking too fast for this long slog of a hike through rough terrain. She'd learned a lot about hiking in the nine months she'd been in Alaska. "And the federal government wants to allow logging? How?"

"Tongass is a big place," Jonas replied. "So not exactly here, but on Prince of Wales Island, to the south of Sitka. It's bigger. Logging was a big industry in the southeast until the early 1990s. Sitka had a big mill, run by the Japanese. In its heyday it employed 500 people. Shipped a ton of lumber to Japan to rebuild there after WWII, and to produce rayon of all things."

Jonas walked a bit in silence, then continued, "But demand fell off, and there were safety issues at the mill. Then environmental groups realized what a unique place the Tongass was and fought to protect it. In 1980, a law was passed protecting the Tongass from logging."

"And the mill closed," Dace said, prompting him.

"Took ten years, but yes. Oddly, it didn't hurt Sitka as much as people thought it would. Tourism, in no small part because of the Tongass, began to grow. It's the major industry in town now. Everything revolves around tourism."

"Mixed blessing?" Dace asked.

"Yeah, isn't everything?"

Paul broke the silence that followed. "Unfortunately, by the time the laws protecting the forest were established, a lot of the old growth was gone. Some estimated 70 percent. What remains is remoter spots like this one."

Dace frowned. "And then what happened? How can the U.S. Forest Service just turn around and decide to start leasing again?"

Jonas snorted. "It's the feds, who knows?"

"Aren't you working for them?" Dace asked.

"No, I'm state, with Fish and Game. Different folks. At least the people who are making the decisions have been here," he replied.

"So, logging?" she asked.

"Word has it, the decision is going to get blocked by the courts," Jonas replied. "At least we're hoping so. There is so much unique habitat out here. Not to mention the salmon industry can't afford to lose the salmon spawning grounds. Logging wouldn't be small scale outfits like it was in the 1950s. They want to come in and build roads, really tear shit up. And it would destroy the streams where the salmon go to spawn."

"And salmon fishing is a huge industry," Paul added.

"Yeah. You ought to get old Swede going on the logging permits sometime," Jonas laughed.

"Swede still around?" Paul asked, then added for Dace's benefit, "He owns the fish packing plant in town. He, and Ben Daniels who owns the bars, and Duke Campbell, the police chief, have run this town forever."

Jonas grunted. "And one of them, if not all of them, are responsible for killing Dad."

"I thought Hank Petras killed him," Dace said, puzzled. "Isn't that why you supposedly killed him?"

"As Paul said, nothing happens in this town without the knowledge, and probably direction, of one of those three people. Petras was the weapon. I want to know who ordered it. And why," Jonas said. "And I didn't kill Petras."

That was a conversation stopper, Dace, thought, and she focused on their downhill scramble in silence.

It took them two hours, but the trail led where they expected, a watering hole. Dace didn't hesitate but walked right into it. She put her face down, and using her hands to scoop up water, she took large gulps.

It felt good. She didn't mind being in the water, the rain had soaked her pretty well. It wasn't a harsh rain, just a persistent, even, warm rain that soaked into the ground and into her. She looked at the men standing next to her, drinking water as she did.

"Do you recognize this place?" she asked Jonas.

Jonas hesitated, then nodded. "Good news is I know where we are."

"And the bad news is?" Paul asked.

"I was right; we're in the vicinity of where I spent the last week mapping." He hesitated again. Dace had been strong so far, a real trooper. He didn't want to break her spirit. But damn, they just didn't get a break. "We're not on Baranof Island," he said reluctantly. "We're on a small, unnamed island, to the northeast of Baranof. That's why I was there — because we don't have good maps of it. My notes are in the office, and those are the first map information this island has ever had."

"Not even tribal maps?" Paul asked.

Jonas shook his head. "It really doesn't have much to offer. It isn't very big. Maybe 100 square miles, and most of it in that peak. It doesn't support much game. Nothing big. No significant minerals show up." He shrugged.

Dace frowned, trying to wrap her brain around it. "It's hard for me to imagine," she said. "How can it not be on the maps? At least for navigation if nothing else."

Jonas nodded. "Oh, it is on those maps," he assured her. "A squiggly shape that tells boats to go around it."

A boom. Gunshot, Dace identified, as she hit the ground. The day had been so silent, that it sounded particularly loud. Rifle? she wondered. It sounded more like the gun Paul carried at work. Which made no sense. Why would there be someone out here shooting a pistol?

"What the f—!" Jonas exclaimed. He, too, flattened himself behind some reeds.

Paul was silent, moving toward the forest where the shot came from almost before Dace had figured out what it was. Most people ran from a gunshot — it would take the shooter a minute to adjust to someone running toward him. Not that Dace intended to follow him. Instead, she belly-crawled backwards, into the tule reeds where Jonas was.

Jonas looked at her. "Will you be OK if I circle around?"

Dace nodded. It would be like flushing dinner last night, she thought, as she watched him head out at an angle to where the shot came from. Of course, there was no reason to believe that the shooter was still there. She slowly backed a bit farther into the reeds.

No lack of water now, she thought with a giggle as she knelt among the reeds in the water. She was cold, but she held still waiting for an all-clear signal from someone.

But the voice she heard wasn't one she recognized.

"Well, look here," said a stranger. "You're not a Kitka. Who are you?"

Dace looked up from her hiding spot. A man in his late 50s knelt on the bank above her. He was looking a bit grizzled, but Dace didn't think he'd been out here that long. She had never seen him before.

"Dace Marshall," she answered. "Who are you?"

"Sitka police," he replied. "Hank Petras."

She looked at him blankly. "You're supposed to be dead."

"Yeah, Hank," Jonas said, from behind him. "What are you doing here?"

The man whirled, bringing his service weapon up. "Jonas Kitka," he said. "They said they'd be dropping you off."

Jonas looked at Dace. "*Run!*" he said.

Dace ducked around Hank Petras, who grabbed for her and missed. And she ran. Wet and cold now as well, she darted for the cover of the trees. She heard the gun go off, but she didn't look back. If he shot at her, he missed. If he shot at someone else, there was nothing she could do for them.

Nothing but stay free of the man who was supposed to be dead.

She hid behind a downed tree, its girth almost as tall as she was. It was covered in moss, like most of the downed trees. Behind it, large-leafed shrubs — thimbleberry, she thought — had colonized, taking advantage of the protected microclimate. Water pooled on their leaves. It was raining steadily now. She shivered. Hypothermia was a real fear now. She needed to get dry, or at least dryer. To find something to protect her from the wet. She inspected the downed tree, and then, dropping to her knees, she began to hollow out a protected spot beneath it.

Jonas reached for Hank's gun while he was distracted by Dace's escape, but Hank was fast. He pointed his weapon at Jonas's head.

"Shall we talk?" he invited. "Who else is out here? You weren't alone coming down that trail."

From their left, Paul said, "I'm here, too, Petras."

"Let's talk, shall we?" Petras said. "Then I'll tell you what you're going to do for me."

"Do for you?" Jonas said. "Why would I do anything for you? They think I killed you."

Petras laughed. "Yeah. Well, we'll get to that."

Petras gestured with his chin. "I've got a camp over that way. Call in the lady. She's going to be awfully cold and wet out there."

"Suppose we talk first," Paul said. "You can tell us what you want, and then we'll talk about Dace."

Jonas moved silently to the left and in front. Hank kept his weapon trained on him. Paul stayed just out of his visual range, but as long as the weapon was trained on his brother, it was more caution on his part than because he was going to try to do something.

And as long as Dace stayed free and could take care of herself, he had options. Not many. But options.

Chapter 20

(The Tongass. Wednesday.)

Paul looked with appreciation around the camp Petras had made. He hadn't even seen it until they were practically in it. Petras had started with a tent, added branches to hide it. He had water jugs, secure food storage, and a fire pit, all hidden behind a blind much like those used for hunting.

Who was he hiding from? Paul wondered.

Hank gestured toward the fire pit, using his chin again.

"Jonas, you probably know how to start that fire," he directed.

Jonas moved silently toward it, found matches, and lit the fire. He found coffee makings and put that to boil over the fire. Paul sat down, still staying as far to Petras' right as he could. He wanted to fragment his focus, to make it so that Petras couldn't have him and Jonas in a single frame.

He gratefully took the cup of coffee that Jonas handed him. Jonas took a second cup and offered it to Petras, who rolled his eyes. Jonas moved out of the frame to Petras' left. Good man, Paul thought. It wasn't that Petras didn't know what they were doing. It didn't matter. You never wanted the guy with the gun to have you grouped.

"I hated your father, and I hated your family," Hank Petras said conversationally. "If your father hadn't been so goddam noble, I wouldn't have been told to shoot him. I knew then that the day would come when I would be disposable. That I would take the fall, and they would walk away."

He looked at them, saw their baffled expressions. "You don't have a clue what I'm talking about, do you?"

Paul shook his head. "Why don't you tell us?"

"You don't remember? Nothing?"

"Remember what?" Paul asked.

Petras snorted. "Holding our breath all these years, and you don't remember a f-cking thing."

"Me?" Paul asked. "What should I remember?"

Petras seemed to want to talk. Paul tried to focus and listen.

"Your father was asking for an investigation into the deaths of two Indians who had died in the jails here. Duke had managed to bluff his way out of it, but the pressure was growing. Your father wouldn't let it go. This was in the late '70s-early '80s, and there was a lot of talk about Native rights. For the chief to hang some AIM guys...." He shook his head.

"Why did he do that?" Jonas asked. "Karin said her father wasn't into violence, at all. Why kill him and make it look like suicide?"

Petras shook his head. "First came the riot, then the jail suicides. Panicked, I guess. Campbell does a lot of that. Ben Daniels? Now that's a stone-cold killer. Remember, this isn't too long after Wounded Knee."

Petras paused, looked off into the woods where Dace had gone to ground. Paul asked a question to bring his attention back.

"So, start with the protest," he said. "What was that about?"

Petras looked back at him, paced some more. "Before my time, of course, but the way I understand it, the tribal council was upset over police treating Native men too roughly." From Petras' tone of voice, he wasn't all that concerned about how Native men were treated. "So, they invited the police chief to meet with them. He didn't take it well, but he showed up and laid down the law to the council. As he and his officers were leaving the meeting, they walked into a protest. Turned into a real mob scene, but the officers were armed and the Natives only had knives, and as you know from current situation, a gun overrules a knife every time."

Paul didn't meet his brother's eyes. Not every time.

"The chief ordered officers to break up the protestors. It got ugly. Most of the Natives carried knives, and when the officers started shoving the picketers, it turned violent. Someone shoved an elderly woman down, and it got completely out of control. Twenty-some were arrested, three Natives and two officers had to be taken to the hospital."

Paul looked at Jonas, raised an eyebrow. Did he know this history? Jonas shook his head. Probably wasn't even born yet.

"When was this?" he asked.

"Oh 1982 or so," Hank said. "You were about four."

Now why would he know that? Paul wondered.

"So anyway, the district attorney out of Juneau intervened, and made Campbell release everyone. Freedom of speech and all that. He did — begrudgingly, I bet — but he refused to let the two go who he claimed were outside agitators."

"How do you know all this?" Jonas asked. "You weren't in Sitka then."

"I made it my business to know," he said. "How do you think I'm still living? They know I've got the goods on them."

Paul frowned. "So, what do you mean, I don't remember?"

"Your father was going to testify before this task force investigation into the deaths. There would be a lot of media interest. Your father wouldn't back down. So, the chief had you kidnapped."

"*What*?!" Paul exclaimed. "How would I forget that?"

Petras shrugged. "You were four. Traumatized. The memory gets blocked. I dunno. It never occurred to any of us that you wouldn't remember." He looked at Paul suspiciously, getting up close in his face.

Paul didn't flinch. Petras grunted and started pacing again.

"How long was I kidnapped?"

"A few days? A week?" Petras shrugged. "It was made clear to your father that he needed to shut up or he'd see you next as a dead body. And if he thought about talking again, he needed to remember how easy it had been to take you the first time."

"So, he backed down."

"Yeah. Hard choice for a noble man," Petras stopped pacing and laughed. "Noble man, get it?" No one else laughed.

"Then you were returned to your parents. And your dad stopped pushing for the investigation. Business went on as usual — just the way Duke Campbell wanted it."

"Except Dad became a drunk," Paul said bitterly.

"When he couldn't handle the choice he had to make, he'd drink," Petras agreed. "And he'd talk. But he couldn't say much, because he didn't know for sure who had been involved. Oh, he guessed the chief had to be, but he had no proof."

"And then one night at the Club, he overheard Ben Daniels talking, and he recognized the voice," Jonas guessed.

"Yeah, don't know what set that off, really, but someone freaked. Ben had a couple of his thugs grab Luke. Shot him up with drugs, and then turned him loose with a gun on the road to the ferry terminal at commute time. Luke was weaving around, waving his hands, trying to get someone to stop and help him. I don't think he's even aware he's got a gun in his hand. Doesn't know where he is, what's going on, poor bastard. All he knows is that he knows who kidnapped you when you were just a little guy."

"And you're sent out to answer the call and tidy things up — nice and legal." Jonas said. Paul was stunned. "It wasn't the first time you'd done things for the chief, was it?"

"No, and it wasn't the last. But I knew bad times were coming," Petras said. He began humming to himself. "I started building me a survival kit. Info to blackmail them into not coming after me. Documents for a new life elsewhere. Money. Takes time. Wanted to finish raising my own family first."

"So, you were going to "die" and start over?" Paul asked.

"Yeah. Then two things happen. One, the chief announces he's thinking about retirement, and he's got this new assistant police chief who thinks he's hot shit. The guys are old. Ben has turned his businesses over to his sons, and they're mostly legal. Swede is hanging in there, running the packing sheds, but he's about done. And he's been mostly legal since the labor unions won against him. Things are winding down, and they're thinking retirement in Florida or Mexico. The old days are just that. Old days."

"And the other thing? Jonas here meets a girl. Turns out the girl isn't just any old girl, but the daughter of one of the men they killed all those years ago. She wants to find out who killed her father and why. And Jonas decides to help her."

Petras paced back and forth by the fire. "And the three of them saw their warm retirement going up in smoke. So, they decided to make my death real, blame Jonas, and it can all be made to go away."

Jonas and Paul looked at each other silently.

"And what's your plan now?" Paul asked. "Seems you've always had a plan."

"Yeah, I got a plan," he said. "I still got the money and the papers, and people think I'm dead. So, I still got a plan. Only thing is...," he trailed off mumbling.

"Only thing is?" Paul prompted.

"My new papers and my money are in town. Don't think the folks are going to believe I'm a ghost do you? Now I need someone to go to town and get my papers out of the safe deposit box at Alaska National Bank. That's where you guys come in."

"They aren't going to give us the papers of a dead man," Jonas protested.

"Well, see, I've got someone who will help me. You don't think I'm in this alone, do you? I have a partner. Fortunately, he'll be along shortly, so we don't have to keep up this friendly little chat for long."

"That sounds like my cue," said a voice behind Paul. He whirled around. The man looked familiar. Someone from last night? Two nights ago, he amended.

"Mike Anderson. I thought I saw you the other night. What are you doing mixed up with Petras?" Jonas said.

The chief's son-in-law, Paul remembered. Former Coast Guard, now police officer. And co-conspirator? Didn't make a lot of sense.

Anderson moved like a fighter. He was light on his feet, balanced to be able to move. He had a rifle slung over his shoulder. He was younger, and in much better shape, than the 50-year-old Petras.

Paul had been pretty sure he and Jonas could take Petras, even if he did have a gun. Things were different now. He wished he'd jumped Petras earlier. But he needed information as much as anything.

Well, that, and a way off the island. Speaking of, he eyed Anderson speculatively. How had he gotten here? Was there a boat somewhere? He hadn't heard a plane, but a boat? A boat would be just fine.

"Well, well, the gang's all here," Mike Anderson said as he slid his gun off his shoulder and moved toward the campfire. He poured himself a cup of coffee. Blew on it, like a man used to the too-hot coffee of a campfire. He looked around the camp and frowned.

"Where's the girl?" he demanded.

"She got away," Petras said sourly. "She can't go far. And she's a complete novice to Alaska, if I read her right."

In exasperation, Anderson exhaled hard through tight lips. "They weren't even supposed to be able to make it off that mountain top," he complained. "Then you radio me and tell me you've spotted them headed your way. So, I come out here to finish the job, because you won't, and there's one running loose!" He ended his tirade on a shout.

Petras shrugged. "Life sucks."

Jonas snorted.

Petras looked over at him. "Not as much for me, as it does for you," he said.

Paul shook his head. "I don't know about that, Hank," he said. "Somehow I don't see him leaving you alive if he kills us in front of you."

Hank grinned. "You're the bright one, aren't you," he said, then shrugged. "But see, I have something he wants very badly."

"Shut up, Hank!" Andrews said with real menace.

"Why? They aren't going anywhere. You're not going anywhere until I've got what I want. If I want to finally tell them why they're going to die, what difference does it make?"

Paul leaned back a bit as if he was relaxed, although he was anything but.

"I don't get it, Hank," he admitted. "I never heard you were a stupid man. Duke's henchman, maybe, but then, he's the police chief, and you're one of his officers, so that's almost legit.

"So how did you end up out here, on an isolated island, with no way off, without the papers you've carefully built over years? It doesn't seem like a well thought out exit."

Hank snorted. "No shit."

Chapter 21

(Sitka, Tongass National Forest. Petras' story. The previous Wednesday, April 1)

The Sitka Orienteering Club had about 20 members but given that few of them worked a regular 8-5 Monday-Friday schedule, it varied how many showed up for a camping expedition. This trek had four people, a smaller than normal group, but not unusually so. Anderson was the trek master for the April trip.

"April Fool's Day. And I was the fool," Hank said, sardonically. Then resumed his description of the trip.

Anderson's job was to pick a site, organize the camping part of it, especially the food and the booze, and make the arrangements for them to be lifted out to the site and then picked back up.

"You know how orienteering works?" Hank asked.

Paul shook his head, but Jonas shrugged. "A bunch of guys doing for fun what I do for a living. Only with alcohol."

Hank laughed. "Close, at that."

The men were dropped in at different locations with a compass and a list of directions for the daily rendezvous. If they did everything correctly, they'd end up at a rendezvous point. They'd eat dinner, drink, tell stories, drink some more. Do it again the next day.

The first day went just as the previous trips Hank had been on. He'd been one of the club's founders of the club ten years ago, and although he didn't make all the trips, he made most of them. Everyone got to the rendezvous point in good time. Dinner was good. He was tired enough to sleep well.

The next morning, Mike handed out the new itinerary. This time, the itinerary was in two parts, one led each man somewhere different, with an object to be found, then a second set of instructions led them all to the evening rendezvous.

But when Hank reached his first location around 2 p.m., Mike was waiting for him.

"What are you doing here?" Hank asked, perplexed. He was a bit later than he'd hoped to be. He had to backtrack some to find the correct route. He was hungry for the lunch in his backpack. And he had no reason to be wary of the man, anyway.

So, he hadn't expected Mike to swing a shovel at him. He'd managed to dodge it, but Mike was 20 years younger and took him down quickly.

"Hard to kill a man with a shovel," Hank told his audience. Mike rolled his eyes.

Concussed and bleeding, Hank rolled away from Mike and pulled out a gun from his backpack. He pointed it at Mike.

"What the hell is going on!" he yelled.

Mike just grinned. "What do you think is going on? Duke wants you dead. I'm his new hatchet man."

"What? Why?"

Mike shrugged. "He's cleaning up loose ends, I guess. And you know a lot of his secrets. He's obsessed with Kitka's new Indian squaw, and he wants you dead, and Kitka disgraced."

"He wants that girl of Kitka's?" Petras asked, honestly confused. The concussion didn't help.

Mike Anderson rolled his eyes. "Don't be stupid. He wants her to go home. He wants you dead. He figures to take Kitka out while he's at it."

"And how does this do that?"

Mike laughed. "Jonas is on a mapping job out here. His GPS tracking data should have him going over the top of your route sometime this morning. He's gone on, of course. He's got a lot of territory to map before they pick him up on Friday."

"OK," Petras said slowly.

"So, I'm going to meet at the rendezvous point as planned. We'll be quite alarmed when you don't show up, but we'll backtrack in the dark to where you're supposed to have gone, and so sad, there's your dead body."

"And what do you get out of all of this?"

"Besides my father-in-law's good will?"

"Yeah, besides that," Hank said, although as he well knew that was considerable all by itself.

"Duke will be retiring in five years," he said. "And he's promised to do all in his power to make me his successor."

Also, doable, and a considerable benefit. He looked at the younger man.

"You ever killed someone before?" he asked. "It isn't as easy as the television shows make it look."

Mike Anderson just grinned.

So, he had. Hank was getting shaky. Holding a gun on someone wasn't as easy as the TV shows made it look either.

"What if I could promise you a faster track to police chief than five years?" Hank asked. "What if you could be chief in six months?"

Mike Anderson stilled. Ahhhh, I've got him, Hank thought with satisfaction.

"That interest you? What if I told you I have enough evidence on your father-in-law for you to make your name as a whistleblower. Then, police chief. And you're young; you could ride it all the way to the statehouse."

Anderson snorted. "And why would you do this for me? I just tried to kill you."

"Because I want you to do something for me, of course. Besides not kill me, I mean." Hank eyed the younger man for a moment, and then continued. "I have enough money to disappear. I was planning to do it in the next year, before your father-in-law retired anyway. This moves my timeline up some. So, you need to take your crew — I assume they're all in on it? — back to town and carry through your plan. Then you need to come back out here with a plan to get me off the island, with my new identity, and the funds from my safety deposit box."

"I could just kill you, then find all your documents," Mike threatened.

Hank smiled gently. "First, I have a gun pointed at you, not the other way around. And second, don't you know Duke has been looking for those documents for years without success? You think you can find them without me?"

Mike Anderson looked at him consideringly, and Hank held his eyes — and his weapon — steady. *Never let them see you flinch* was a mantra he'd been practicing for a long time.

"Deal," he said. "We've got a deal."

Chapter 22

(Tongass. Present day. Wednesday.)

Dace looked at the space she'd dug and shook her head. The rain was getting worse. She'd be in the mud, and though the tree would give her some protection, it wouldn't keep her warm.

Also, she didn't know what was happening. Paul and Jonas could be dead. Or, they could have killed that man and were looking for her. Or who knew what else?

So, she reconsidered her options. She'd lived alone outside Talkeetna for a while last year. But she'd had all the gear she needed. Here she had nothing.

And waiting wasn't going to put her in a better situation. She'd just be colder. Wetter. Hungrier.

If she was going to do something, there was never a better time than now. She got up, used some of the moss to clean the mud off her hands.

Hank had to have come to this island somehow, she thought. How did he get here? She moved silently through the woods back to the clearing, and then around the clearing to the other side. This was the island Jonas had been mapping, she thought, so he'd come and gone from it as well. That spoke of a dock somewhere.

She pushed her way through the woods moving downhill, never a bad strategy she knew. And then she broke through the woods to a beach. It startled her. The sand was pristine white; it could be on a postcard. The dark blue waves crashed against it. She watched for a while, decided she must be on the inland side, because there didn't seem to be any tide movement. Although, there could be tides on the leeward side, she thought doubtfully. But if there wasn't tide movement? Had to be inland.

She shrugged. If it was inland, then the south would be to her right. Jonas had said they were north, northeast of Sitka. She stayed to the edge of the forest and headed south.

Sure enough, about an hour walk, she thought an hour, no way to tell, she spied what looked like a dock. And a shed. She could have cried at the sight. She started jogging toward it, and then realized that was a motor she heard.

"Damn it," she said out loud, dropping to her knees behind a tree. Who would that be? Someone looking to rescue them?

Or someone looking to finish them off?

A motorboat pulled up alongside the dock, and a man jumped out, killing the motor. Young, fit, Dace thought. Probably about her own age. She couldn't get a good look at him, and he was wearing the ubiquitous slicker, hat and boots Sitkans seem to wear a lot. Sitka sneakers, she thought, snickering at what the rubber boots were called. She sobered up. Giggles were not a good sign.

Dace worked her way closer, trying to get a better look at the man. She didn't recognize him. She was pretty sure she didn't recognize him.

Still, he wasn't a Coastie, as Jonas, called them, or the boat would be marked. And it wasn't a police boat either. On the other hand, he was probably too tall to be an Alaska Native. She'd feel more comfortable if he were Alaska Native. So far, all the bad guys in this mess had been white.

She stayed hidden. The man pulled a rifle out from the boat and shouldered it. OK, that clinched it. She wasn't going to go running out there thinking she was saved.

No reason not to be cautious and watch for a little while longer before she revealed herself.

The man strode up the beach as if he knew where he was headed. He didn't walk as if he thought he had to worry about anyone, Dace thought from her spot hidden among the trees. So, either he doesn't know about Hank Petras, or he's an ally. And he doesn't seem to expect to find Jonas or Paul either, she realized.

Of course, he could be a hunter who was clueless to the drama that was being played out just beyond the trees. Dace considered and discarded that. If he was, there was nothing she could do for him. And she didn't think he was a big game hunter. Wouldn't they drop onto the peak? It was a long, up-hill hike from here. As she well knew, and she'd been going downhill.

Dace watched him until he disappeared up a trail that she'd failed to see. Confirms he knows where he's going, she thought.

She slipped out of the bushes, and back onto the beach. Moving at a fast trot she headed for the boat. She hadn't ever driven one, but she figured it wouldn't be any more difficult than a plane. She peered in, took a look up the coast, and then slid into the driver's seat.

"Shit," she muttered, as she eyed the ignition switch. It needed a key. For some reason, she had assumed it wouldn't. She rummaged around in the various nooks and crannies around the steering wheel to see if there was a spare hidden somewhere.

There wasn't.

There was an oar in the back. But Dace didn't even try to lift it out. She wouldn't have the upper body strength to paddle a boat this size. She'd done a bit of canoeing, and she knew what it took. Add in that she didn't know where she was, didn't know where Sitka was from here, and that it could well be open ocean between here and there? No, she wasn't going to paddle out.

And casting a wistful look at the empty ignition, she wasn't going to drive it out. She considered cutting it lose, but, knowing that there was a way off the island even if she couldn't use it right now was better than being completely stranded.

"OK," she muttered out loud. "Next up, that shed."

The shed was about 8 feet by 8 feet, with a solid roof. And it was padlocked. She tugged at it, knowing Lanky's habit of not quite locking padlocks tight because he didn't want to find the key for it later. But it was locked.

She sighed. Nothing was going to be easy on this trip. Just fly her friend down to his hometown to see his mom on her maiden voyage. Piece of cake. She sighed again.

She examined all the sides of the building, and on the side that backed up to the forest she found what she was looking for — a loose board. She trotted back down to the boat to find something that she could use as a crowbar and returned with a boat hook. It was metal, about six feet long, with a hook on one end. Dace wondered what boaters used it for. It looked fairly lethal. She eyed it again, considering. She might take it back with her.

But first, she wanted inside the shed.

Using the boat hook, she was able to pry off the loose board, and then, with one board gone, the others around it came off easily. She crawled inside.

It was pitch black dark, except for the bit of light coming in from the hole she'd just created. Of course it's dark, she thought sourly. Nothing about this could be easy. She gingerly felt along the wall, giving her eyes time to adjust.

She found the counter by bumping into it.

"Ouch!"

She paused, waiting for the pain in her shin to subside a bit, and then realized she could see the faint outline of the shapes on the bench. And one of the shapes was a lantern. Fortunately, whoever had stocked the shed, had provided a battery-powered one, because if she'd needed to light an oil lamp, she was out of luck.

She flipped the lantern's switch and could see around in the shed. For a moment she just stared. Then she sent a fervent request for blessings upon whoever stocked the shed. There were foodstuffs, slickers, even a cache of sweats of varying sizes. All of them too large for her, but she didn't care. She stripped out of her wet clothing and pulled them on. She hungrily ate the energy bars until she felt satisfied and stopped shivering. Now dry and fed, she felt like she could think clearly again.

Jonas seemed to think she needed to stay free, but on reconsideration, she wondered if he hadn't just been unnecessarily protective. She was unexpected. The kidnappers had meant to just grab the two Kitkas, and she didn't think anyone had told Petras that she was along.

At the same time, if they did know about her, why bother to look? She'd come to Alaska because it was so very easy to die out here. Just pick a trail and eventually something will get you. The weather, the wildlife, the terrain. Something.

So, she had choices. And that meant she needed to figure out her goals.

Dace considered that as she rummaged through the energy bars looking for a chocolate one. She no longer needed nutrients, but chocolate was always a morale booster.

Was her goal to get back to Sitka? Yes.

To be with Paul? She shied away from that question. Yes. The memory of their exploration that morning made her blush. But yes, she was reluctant to leave him. Not just because she was worried about him and what Petras and the mystery man had in mind, but because she didn't trust what they had enough to look away. If you looked away, it might change. And the man you thought you knew? Wasn't what or who you thought he was.

Paul is nothing like my husband, she said silently, repeating it like a mantra. She knew he wasn't. Really, she did.

They'd been sharing a house for nine months now. She knew him. She knew what he ate for breakfast. She knew about his collection of knives and his collection of books about Alaska. She knew he was committed to his job. Drove too fast. That he genuinely liked people but was content with his own company most of the time.

That he was gentle. Patient. Kind. Not just with her but with everyone. She'd seen him interact with the Abbott children and knew he loved kids.

And yet? She was obviously a bad judge of people to have married her ex. Of course, he'd been a sociopath who had fooled some of the biggest names in politics — people who weren't easily fooled because they were sociopaths, too.

She wanted Paul.

Just admitting that to herself made her not only blush but want to run like a scared rabbit.

After all, what if they tried for something more, and it failed, and she lost the only friend she had?

Well, that sounded pathetic, she scolded herself. And it wasn't true. She had a dozen or more friends in Talkeetna, an amazing richness of friends for a woman who never had a real friend before. But she knew that losing Paul's friendship would break her.

"Buckle up," she murmured. Obviously, her friendship with Paul had already passed into something more than a friendship.

"Enough." She said that out loud as well. She needed to figure things out.

But really? She knew she didn't know enough about boats to steal one and head into unknown open waters. A plane, now? Sure. But not a boat. She couldn't just sit here and wonder what was happening. Now it was time to take her trusty boat hook and head back to where she'd last seen Petras with her friends. And see if she could set about freeing them, then find out what the hell was going on.

She found a ratty backpack that someone had discarded in the corner. It looked like the drab green one Lanky had in the hangar, she thought. He'd probably had it since he mustered out after WWII. This one smelled even mustier. She sighed. She was getting used to the litter piles found in Alaska. Disposing of garbage was expensive. Couldn't bury it in much of the state, because of permafrost. Alaskans tended to discard what they no longer needed wherever it stopped being useful. To their credit, they tended to use something to the very last ounce of possibility. Reduce, reuse, recycle had been an Alaska way of life long before it became a trendy motto for recycling in the Lower 48.

So, the good news was you found things like musty backpacks in forgotten buildings. The bad news, she thought morosely, was that they had already been used to the last drop.

And that phrase reminded her of coffee and that it had been a long time since her last cup. She scowled.

She had to use some plastic from the boxes of energy bars and water bottles to line the backpack — it had more holes than solid parts — and she was beginning to wonder if it was worth the time she was spending on it.

"I'm procrastinating," she said out loud. "It's wet and cold out there. There are men with guns. And I want to go home and have coffee, not go back out there looking for my men."

She pushed the backpack out the hole she'd made, and then slid out the boathook. She peered out first, then slithered out herself. "Be my luck to crawl out into the hands of one of the bad guys," she muttered. "Or a bear. Did Jonas say there were bear here? Probably."

With that thought, she carefully closed off the hole. No use letting varmints of any size get inside. They might not be able to get back out. And she just might need a bolt hole again.

She slung the backpack over her shoulder and picked up the boathook, which she discovered made a pretty good walking staff. And then she moved up into the fringe edge of the forest and started making her way back toward the pond and Petras' camp.

Chapter 23

Back at Petras' camp, Mike grunted. "I had to kill a deer to get enough blood. Took samples from him, and his bloody clothes."

"I didn't think deer blood was going to work. Deer blood isn't going to fool any crime scene inspector," Hank said.

"But I am the crime scene inspector," Mike said, obviously pleased with himself. "No body, but given we were all cops this trip, who's going to question us?"

Hank looked over at Paul and rolled his eyes. Obviously, Hank had given some thought to who might be along to question it, even if Anderson hadn't. Of course, Paul had been long gone from Sitka when Mike had arrived on the scene.

Mike threw his cup at the log Paul was sitting on and swore viciously.

"Went just like we planned. Until Monday when Seth Jones insists on seeing his client. And then who shows up in town but Kitka's big brother, the state patrol lieutenant? And I think, we're screwed."

So, he'd hightailed it out to talk to Petras, Monday, and then back to town to kidnap the three and call in a favor from his Coast Guard buddies to help dispose of them.

"Burned a lot of gas in that boat of yours," Jonas said.

Petras laughed. "Oh yeah. Mike's been having to scramble big time over this. But until he gets my money and papers, I'm not giving him a damn thing."

Petras looked at Mike with disdain. "Why do I think you don't have them this trip either?"

"Bank refused to open up the box," Mike Anderson said angrily. "Said until an inquest ruled on your death, they would wait. Especially without a body."

Paul saw the way Mike looked at Petras, and he knew Petras saw it too. Mike was preparing to deliver Petras' body. Along with Dace and Jonas and his own. Kill all of them, and he could be the hero, and spin the story however he wanted.

Paul didn't think his own boss would buy it, but it wouldn't matter if he were dead.

Petras started laughing. "Problem with that, son...my money and new identity papers are in that box. But not the evidence you want to bring Duke down. That's in a different place. So, if you're thinking about hauling my body into town, rethink that. Because you won't get what you want."

Mike swore some more.

Paul instinctively felt some motion. When he looked up his eyes widened to see Dace swing a boat hook at Mike's head and dang near knock him out.

Jonas sprang up, grabbed Mike, tossed his weapon to Paul, and put Mike in a chokehold before he could shake off his dazed reaction to Dace's blow.

Petras just laughed. Then he turned sober and pointed his gun at Dace. "Unh-uh," he said, shaking his head at Paul. "Put the gun down, Paul. And you might get some rope and tie Mike up before he gets loose from Jonas there. There's some rope stored behind the food container."

"As if," Jonas grunted. But Mike twisted, forcing Jonas to tighten his hold. "But rope would be good."

Paul looked at Petras warily and decided that yes, he was capable to shooting Dace first, if he felt threatened. He dropped the gun where he was standing and went to fetch the rope.

Hank moved quickly. He reached for Dace and dragged her to him. She didn't try to fight him. Hank Petras had a firm grip on her neck, and the gun was held tightly against the base of her jaw. She let him use her as a shield.

For now, she thought grimly. There's always an opening... even against an armed opponent with nothing to lose.

She wasn't sure if she'd improved matters with her attack on Mike Anderson. Maybe not, because now she was caught and helpless. But it had felt good to whack the man who had kidnapped her. It was too bad the boat hook hadn't been heavier. But then, if it had been, she wouldn't have been able to lug it all the way back.

Dace held herself still. Don't make sudden moves around angry men.

Her husband, now deceased, had taught her many lessons about surviving angry men. No sudden moves. Stay silent if you can. Don't defy them. Don't meet their eyes.

Also, it is always your fault. Even if you don't know what you did, it is always your fault. Don't bother to protest, don't question. Just accept responsibility and the blame. And the punishment. And the blame for forcing him to punish you.

He's dead, she reminded herself. Except sometimes he lived in her head. She could hear his cold, precise voice, the voice only she ever heard. His clients and his employees got a warm, passionate voice. An offer of friendship and collegiality, of belonging.

She, who wanted to belong to someone so badly, wasn't offered that. She was something to be owned. And that was a world of difference.

So, what did Hank Petras want, she thought dispassionately. What did he want from her? Something. He wanted something from her, not just Paul and Jonas. Something, or he'd have shot her, she thought. She didn't know why she thought that. But she knew angry men, and she knew he'd have shot her and buried her in the tule weeds if he didn't need her.

Even if it was just a hostage to ensure the brothers' good behavior, there was something he needed her for. She let out a slow breath. Sooner or later, he'd tell her.

Sooner or later, she'd know what she had to do.

Petras pushed Dace onto a log and moved where he could see them better. He kept his weapon at the ready, but at least it wasn't screwed into Dace's neck any longer. Dace rubbed the spot, more for psychological reasons, than for pain. She caught his eyes on her and gave him a small smile and a slight nod.

The two brothers looked at each other. Dace's eyes were fixed on Petras.

Watching from the forest, she had become uncomfortable with his twitching, the way he trailed off into mumbles at times as he told the story of meeting up with Mike Anderson and the bargain they'd struck. Unbalanced, she thought. Well, someone had tried to kill him. And then he'd negotiated a deal with the man. And now something had gone wrong. But the twitchier he got, the more convinced she had become that she needed to intervene rather than wait any longer.

She looked at the tension building between the two Kitka men. They were calculating the odds of jumping Petras now. But Dace could already figure it: a twitchy man with a gun and nothing to lose almost always wins.

"OK," she said mildly, "Did I smell coffee?"

All three men looked at her with various degrees of astonishment on their faces. She shrugged. "Well, I am going on two days without coffee. That's serious withdrawal territory. It's either coffee, or I will figure a way to shoot someone. So, coffee?"

There was a pause. Then Petras gestured toward the coffee pot. "Jonas, give the lady some coffee."

Jonas poured her a cup then handed it to her. He winked and nodded. She assumed that meant he approved, and she felt better. "Blow on it a bit," he advised. "It's hot."

She blew on it. Took a sip. It was horrible coffee, simply blissful. She closed her eyes and tipped her head back, savoring the first sip.

"Damn," Petras said. "I've seen women have orgasms with less pleasure."

"Respect," Paul growled.

"Nothing disrespectful meant," Petras said. "I'm just not going to get between the lady and her coffee. Ever."

Dace smiled at him. Maybe he wasn't so much a bad guy as a desperate one. Then she remembered he'd killed Luke Kitka on orders. So, he was a desperate bad guy.

Paul stewed. What was it he had forgotten? he wondered. What was he missing?

Mike had stopped struggling and glared. "Untie me you asshole," he said to Petras.

Petras laughed. "She nailed you, a good one, Mike," he said, dropping his gun hand to his side. "Can't say I blame her."

"Should have killed her, left the brothers here to take the fall for her death. Are you going to untie me?"

Hank Petras shrugged. "You're always scheming, making things too complicated, Mike," he said.

"We could simplify things right here," Mike said.

"These two aren't going to go down easy, especially if we make a move to harm her," Petras said.

Mike struggled against the ropes that bound him. "You saying we couldn't take them?" he asked with quiet menace.

Hank shrugged. "One gun. Two of us. Three of them. They'd be fighting for their lives. I didn't get to be this old fighting with those kinds of odds."

He took a sip of coffee. "Besides, I've got options now. I just might want to cut a new deal. The bank won't give you my papers and stash? Then what good are you to me?"

Mike swore and struggled. Paul smiled slowly.

"I can cut you a deal," he said. "A legal one."

Dace grinned at Paul. "I know where there's a boat."

Paul smiled. "So, Petras. You willing to turn state's evidence against Duke Campbell? And Mike here? And all the others?"

Hank Petras hesitated. Paul glared at him. "What?"

"That could tie me up for years," he said. "I was picturing myself in Mexico by winter."

Paul snorted. "I don't think you see your options clearly. It's not Mexico vs testifying for the next two years. It's testifying for the next two years vs serving time for ten."

"When you put it that way," Petras said dryly. "Of course, I could just run."

"And how is that working out for you?" Paul asked. "Because you are trapped on this island, if we leave without you."

Petras paced restlessly.

"Hank," Dace said. "You got kids?"

"Yeah. Two. They're in college," he replied. "That's why I was getting ready to bolt. Wife and I split when the youngest graduated from high school."

Dace nodded. "OK, so you disappear. There will be a standing warrant for your arrest. You can't come back. Can't contact your kids. You'll never know your grandchildren. Is that what you want? Or you delay for a couple of years. Turn state's evidence. Look like a hero. Then go to Mexico. But you're still a part of your kids' lives."

"Grandchildren," he mused. Then sighed and looked at Kitka. "She does the carrot part of the deal better than you do."

"That's because I'm the one with a big stick," Paul replied.

Jonas snickered. Everyone looked at him. "Sorry, it just sounded wrong."

Dace blushed, and Paul laughed.

"OK, OK, state's witness it is. But you've got to protect me," Petras said. "I need out of Sitka as fast as possible or I won't live to testify."

Paul nodded. "You're going to have an armed police escort from now on, Hank," he said. He held out his hand for Hank's gun. Hank surrendered it reluctantly.

"Yeah? Who?"

Paul's grin wasn't kind. "Me."

Petras shook his head, and sighed. "I keep forgetting you're a cop. A Kitka from Sitka is a cop."

Paul looked at Mike Anderson. "Apparently, you're not the only one who struggles with that."

It took very little time for the men to break down camp. Dace was assigned guard duty. She sat with Petras' pistol in her hand and Anderson's rifle at her feet and watched Anderson closely. She could see him tensing and relaxing his arms, flexing his muscles. Trying to stretch the rope, she decided. The rope was just camp rope, more designed for stringing between trees than restraining prisoners, so it was possible it would work. She doubted it, but it was possible. But he'd then have to overpower her, defeat three men, and run. Each more unlikely than the previous step. He'd be better off to wait until they were back in Sitka, where he'd have access to his resources, she thought. But he was angry. He wasn't thinking. She knew the look.

It felt good to have the upper hand for a change.

Petras was nervous and that made Dace nervous. She watched him carefully. Paul's attention was on Mike Anderson. Jonas was running the boat. So, she kept a close eye on Petras.

Hard to know. He was a tightly wired man coming unwound and had been probably since he realized Duke Campbell had sent his son-in-law to kill him. He'd been scrambling to stay alive ever since, and Dace allowed that would wear on a man.

She'd done that for three years of marriage before she escaped. But she considered that Petras had known the day was coming from the first time he did a job off the books for Campbell. He'd done it — whatever that first job was, because killing Luke Kitka wasn't his first — and the clock started ticking for when Duke's paranoia would get to the point that he'd see Hank Petras as a liability instead of a weapon.

She got it. But the nerves Petras was displaying were over the top even for all of that. She narrowed her eyes at him speculatively. What did he have planned, exactly?

It seemed his options were limited. He'd agreed to Paul's terms to turn state's evidence against Duke, and Mike too, she supposed. Buying time, she thought. Buying a way back into town.

Then what? What was he up to?

She admired his craftiness, really. Not everyone could look at a killer and talk their way out of it. Come to think of it, she'd done that too. She considered his jitters in that light.

Yes, he had something planned. For when? And where?

"Where are you going to take us?" Petras asked Jonas.

Jonas looked at Paul. "Good question."

Paul considered. "Moor the boat at that old dock on Sheldon Jackson campus," he said. "We'll take them to Mom's."

"Are you sure that's a good idea? Bringing this to her place?" Jonas asked doubtfully.

"I figure Wyckoff will be in town by now. Her place is the best I can think of to find him."

Hank was all but bouncing with the stress. "You're that confident he'd come here?"

Paul snorted. "You all kidnapped a state patrol officer, and then made me the fall guy for a jail break? You'll be lucky if he doesn't have half the state's patrol officers here. And the FBI. You're so used to controlling everything that happens in this town you've lost sight of the bigger world out there. I realize that Sitka is about five square miles surrounded by reality but get a grip."

"You weren't supposed to survive it," Mike snarled. It was the first thing he'd said since they'd tied him up.

Dace watched the men. Paul had done that to goad him into talking, she decided. Paul was a clever man. Do her well to remember that.

Trust. It always came down to trust. She trusted Paul, she thought, but she needed to remember he was a cop. And that was his first priority, probably always would be. If she got crosswise of that? The law would win, not her. Even with all he'd done last year to see that she got a fair shake, if she'd truly been guilty of her husband's murder, he would have arrested her and never looked back. She was OK with that, she thought. She didn't plan on getting between him and what he thought was right. Of course, a person rarely did plan on doing something stupid like that. It just happened.

Or as her dad used to say, "It probably seemed like a good idea at the time."

Thinking of her father during the good times made her smile.

She looked at each of the men in the boat. They were all plotting things that seemed like good ideas at the time.

She didn't worry about Jonas as much. He wasn't much of a plotter. It was his reactions that got him in trouble. She'd keep that in mind.

Paul? He was plotting how to get to his captain, in whom he had touching faith, she thought. But then, she was equally sure that Lanky was here, or on his way here, to rescue her. And looky there, she'd rescued herself.

Mike Anderson wanted loose, and he wanted the police chief, she thought. He figured Duke would rescue him and make things right. Maybe, but she rather thought Duke Campbell would put himself first. If rescuing Anderson helped Duke Campbell? Then he'd do it. Otherwise, Anderson was a perfect sacrificial lamb. The fall guy.

And that took her back to Hank, who now was not only twitching but humming to himself. She watched him. Cracking up? Or wanting everyone to think he was? Maybe they should have tied him up too.

Jonas slowed the boat as they entered the harbor. Dace let out a breath she didn't know she'd been holding. Tension leached from her body at the signs of human occupancy. A town. Docks, boats. As they got closer, sounds. Cars. All the evidence that they were not alone in the world. She hadn't realized how vulnerable being alone in a wilderness had made her feel. She hadn't been completely alone, at that, but it was as if the rest of the world had disappeared. And now it was back.

Paul smiled at her. "Feels good to be back to civilization, doesn't it?"

She nodded fervently.

But Jonas snorted. "I could stay out there the rest of my life. I don't miss this at all. Not the 'civilization,'" he said, making air quote marks for emphasis, "not the people."

"You'd miss a few people though," Dace observed.

"A very short list," Jonas said. "Very short."

Dace smiled at him, understanding him perfectly. Her list was short too. But she did like "civilization." Especially toilets. Hot showers. Coffee. Clean clothes.

She was thinking about those things when Petras made his move.

Chapter 24

(Sitka harbor. So close! Wednesday afternoon.)

In a fluid, purposeful move, Petras grabbed her and the weapon she held. She struggled, but even though she was 20 years younger, he outweighed her by 50 pounds. He was stronger and had stayed fit.

And as a cop, he was used to controlling a person. She wasn't.

Before anyone could react, he pulled her onto the dock and had the gun pushed up against her chin.

"I'm sorry, girl," he said to her. "But I'm not going to spend two years of my life tied up with a damn fool crusade against Duke Campbell. And I'm not convinced that even with my testimony, Campbell is going down."

Hank Petras looked at Paul. "Good luck with that," he said a bit louder. "I mean that truly. But Duke is a vicious man, and I'm not sure you can protect me, much less win against him. So, I'm bowing out. I'm taking the little lady, getting my stuff, and leaving. I'll send her back with the documents I have on Duke's activities. Maybe that will be enough."

Paul evaluated the situation, calculating his odds. Jonas was helpless to help. He was idling the boat against the dock, but until someone tied off the boat, Jonas couldn't leave the wheel and had a prisoner tied up at his feet. He scrambled mentally for a plan of action and came up with nothing. Petras had the upper hand.

Apparently, Dace had done the same calculation. "It's OK," she told him. "I'll be fine. He doesn't want to hurt me if he doesn't have to."

"She's got that right, Kitka," Petras said, backing down the dock a ways. "So, you all just stay in the boat for 15, and let me go. I'm going to put the gun in my pocket. But don't doubt that I can shoot her faster than you can get to me."

He looked at Mike Anderson. "Say goodbye to your father-in-law for me. Make sure you tell him I refused to testify against him. I don't want him hunting me down either."

"You don't need to worry about him," Anderson said viciously. "Worry about me. Because I'm coming for you, I don't care how long it takes. You better plan to spend the rest of your life looking over your shoulder. And one day? I'll be there."

Hank Petras looked at him for a moment then shrugged. In one motion, he pulled the gun away from Dace's head, and fired a shot. It hit Mike Anderson in the chest.

Paul cursed and dropped to his knees beside his prisoner, putting pressure over the wound. He looked up at Petras. "You'd better run fast," he said.

Hank just smiled, put the gun in his pocket and, pulling Dace with him, set off for the street at the end of the pier.

"You got a plan for what you're doing next?" Dace asked conversationally.

"Yup."

"You going to tell me what it is?"

"Nope. You're just along for the walk, girl. The less you know, the better off you are."

Dace took a few more steps. "I could be helpful if I knew what you had in mind," she said carefully. "You still have to get off Sitka."

"That's down the road," he said. "If there's one thing Sitka has plenty of is pilots who will take cash and ask no questions."

"I'm a pilot," she said.

He looked at her sideways without slowing his pace. He had a destination in mind, she thought. "Are you now? And why would you be willing to help me escape?"

Why indeed, she thought. "Because I don't think your stash of evidence is in Sitka at all," she said, mustering her courage. "I don't think you plan to share it with Paul. And I want the evidence. Duke tried to kill us. I want him to get locked up for a very long time."

"Now how did you figure that out?" he said, laughing.

She shrugged, lengthening her stride to keep up with him. "You're a lot less crazy and a lot wilier than you pretend," she said. "And you've survived under Duke Campbell for 20 years. It's what I would do. You mailed the stuff somewhere else. A Ketchikan mailbox maybe?"

"Good guess," he admitted. "But you still didn't tell me how you'd guessed."

"Because I stole some papers from my husband and blackmailed him to escape," she said. "I know what I did. We're not so different."

"You're that girl!" Petras stopped, looked at her consideringly. "Huh. Maybe we can work a deal."

Dace said nothing more. Petras slowed them to more of a stroll as they left the harbor area and headed into the downtown. Dace wished she wasn't being force-marched along the walkway, so she could look around. Truly Sitka was beautiful. Instead, she kept her eyes straight ahead, and her awareness focused on the man beside her. She wished she knew what he was thinking.

Probably the same thing she was, she thought with amusement. How to stay alive for one more step of the journey.

"OK, now," Petras said conversationally. "You could scream for help. But I'll shoot you, just as I shot Anderson back there. I won't hesitate. You understand that?"

"Yes," she said. And she did.

"Good. Now, we're going to go visit a friend, through the back door of her shop. You're going to stay quiet. She'll help me get to the bank." He looked her over. "You're looking a bit the worse for wear," he observed. "So, you'll stay in the car with my friend. But if you think I'd shoot you? She'd do it faster. And her only regret would be getting the blood out of the seats in her car. Again. Got it?"

"Got it," she said. She felt a bit resentful about the worse for wear comment. She'd flown in from Anchorage, been kidnapped, hiked for two days, fled capture, led an escape, ridden in an open boat for two hours in saltwater spray, and he thought she looked a bit scruffy, did he? She snorted. She didn't even want to think about what she smelled like.

Mike looked at her sideways but didn't question her. Likely he thought she was as crazy as she thought him. She smiled at that.

"Hold it together now," he said cautiously.

She smiled more genuinely at that. "Don't worry. It's not the first time someone has held a gun on me. At least this time, I'll actually know how to fly the plane."

Apparently, he knew her story well enough that he didn't need to ask for an explanation. Or maybe he was so focused on his own needs he didn't care.

Sitka's main street was charming, she decided. She liked Talkeetna, but Sitka was a bit bigger and had more to offer. She wanted to pause at the drum shop. And the bookstore sign up ahead lured her into picking up her pace. A real bookstore!

"Slow down," Petras said with exasperation. "In here."

'Here' was a small shop designed to lure in tourists. A bit of local art, some books, and too many souvenirs to count. It looked interesting enough, she decided. But it was empty. Still too early in the year for the cruise ship to be coming into port. She looked up at the woman approaching to greet them with surprise.

"Not a word," Petras warned.

"What are you doing here?" the woman hissed at them. "You're supposed to be dead!"

"Reports of my death were greatly exaggerated," he said ironically.

"Mark Twain," Dace said, pleased to know the quote. She might be getting a bit loopy, she decided as both of them stared at her for a moment.

"I need your help, and then I'm gone. No one has to know you helped me. Or even saw me."

"What prevents me from picking up the phone and calling 911?" she demanded.

"He's got a gun in his pocket," Dace said helpfully. "I suppose he's willing to use it on you too. He just shot Mike Anderson."

"Hush, now," Petras said with exasperation.

"You shot.... Hank, what the hell are you doing?" the woman said.

"Whatever I have to do to get out of this alive," Hank Petras said grimly. "What is Duke thinking?"

She sighed, troubled. "Isn't that the 64-million-dollar question? OK, what do you need?"

"A ride to the bank. Then a ride to the airport. Dace here is going to fly me out of here, aren't you girl?"

Dace looked at the woman and nodded. She couldn't quite figure out her role in this. Small town. Everyone knew everyone. Everyone knew everyone's secrets. But still.

"OK. Come out this way," she gestured toward the back, and went to lock the front and flip the sign to closed. "No customers this early in the season anyway."

She led them through an office and then a storeroom and out the back door into an alley. The alley was narrow and had seen better days. Or maybe this was as good as it had ever been, Dace thought. There was a small parking spot with an elderly green Volkswagen Rabbit. The woman unlocked the passenger doors, and then went around to the driver's side.

"Put her in back," she said sourly. "We don't want someone spotting her."

"Don't want anyone spotting me either," Petras observed, but he did as she directed. Dace sat in the back, saying nothing. She was trying to figure out the relationship between the two and what that meant for her own survival.

Dace considered that. If she was to survive, the woman needed to think she was a safe witness to leave alive. It didn't matter what was really going on here. What mattered was the story Dace created for her to relax.

The distance to the bank was short. A matter of blocks really. Dace was surprised Hank had even brought the store owner into the mess when they could have easily walked the short distance. But then, they had to get to the airport. So maybe he knew what he was doing.

Hank slid out. "I'll be right back. Don't go anywhere," he warned. "I don't have much to lose at this point."

"Go," the store owner ordered, tapping her well-manicured red nails on the steering wheel.

Hank did, sliding the gun out of his pocket and under the seat.

"We could just drive away," Dace said.

She sighed. "It's complicated. It's really for the best if we get Hank off Sitka and out of here. Did he really shoot Mike Anderson?"

"Yes," Dace said. "But then, I guess, since Mike tried to kill him out on the orienteering weekend, maybe he deserved it."

The woman snorted. "What a f-cked-up mess."

"Must be hard, being in a small town like this when friends get crosswise of each other, and you're caught in the middle," Dace ventured.

The driver looked at her in the rearview mirror. "You know about doing what's needed to survive, don't you?"

"Yes."

The two sat in silence. "So, you're flying Hank out of here? Why?"

"He's kind of had a bum rap," Dace said, and realized she really believed that. "He's been a loyal police officer for decades, and then cops are going to take him out? Looks like he was prepared for that."

"So, you'll betray your cop lover for a man you barely know?"

"Paul's not my lover," Dace said. "But I'm not betraying him. He knows what's going on." She hoped.

The woman snorted and shook her head. "This isn't going to end well for any of us," she predicted, as she started her car and pulled up to let Hank back in the car.

"OK, to the airport. You got a way of starting your plane when we get there?" Hank asked. He pulled the pistol out from under his seat.

"Yes."

They rode in silence across the bridge. Dace was amazed at the view from the top of the high arching bridge. The sun was out, and everything glistened. "It's beautiful here," she said.

"I won't miss it," Hank said. "It's beautiful when the sun is out, but nine months of the year it rains. 120 inches of rain per year. Thirty inches of it in October alone."

"You'll miss it," Dace said.

"Maybe. But I'm headed some place dryer. Warmer. Of course, that describes most of the world outside of Alaska," he said, and cackled.

Their driver dumped them outside the hangar. "Don't come back, Hank," she warned. "And...." She stopped.

"I know," Hank said. "You take care, now. He's gone around the bend, and you're going to be in for a rough time."

"You think I don't know that?" she snapped. And with one last look at Dace and a shake of her head, she sped off the way she came.

"Let's go," Hank said.

Dace found the spare key where Lanky kept it. She did the pre-flight, then checked in with flight control. Hank got jittery.

"Look," she finally snapped. "I'm a novice pilot. This was my first solo flight after getting my license Monday morning. So, calm it down, and let me do this by the book, OK?"

"Shit," he said, tipping his head back against the seat, and banging it. "I'll never make it to Ketchikan."

"That's where we're going?" Dace asked.

"Yeah, you guessed it. I hope your boyfriend doesn't guess it, too."

She hoped he did, but even if he didn't, she'd figure something out.

Once she was in the air, she relaxed. Strange to realize that she'd never been in a small plane until less than a year ago, and now she felt most at home in the air. But this would be a short flight, 40 minutes. Barely enough time to relax at all.

"How did you become Campbell's hatchet man, anyway?" Dace shouted over the sound of the plane.

"I came up here with a wife, a kid, and another one on the way, and not enough money for a plane ticket home if it didn't work out," Petras said. He had a way of pitching his voice to carry through the noise. Maybe he spent more time in planes than she had.

"And I did what my boss said." He shrugged. "By the time I realized he was asking me to do illegal things, it was too late. My wife had made friends. The kids were doing well in school. We were well connected in a church."

He shrugged again. "All cops do what I did to some extent or another. Even your boy scout Paul Kitka. They rough up a suspect a bit to get some information. Or they carry a throw down, just in case."

At her questioning look, he clarified. "An untraceable weapon you carry so that if you do shoot someone and turns out they don't have a gun, well, you can drop it at the scene."

She nodded. Surely Paul didn't do that, she thought doubtfully. She had him on a white horse ready to charge after injustice. Was Petras right that all cops were corrupt to some extent or another? She didn't want to believe that. Bad apples, sure. Justifying his action by claiming everybody does it? Her dad hadn't let her get away with that argument in the second grade.

"And most of those that I roughed up were Natives. Drunk Natives. I didn't really have a problem with that. Drunk Natives are the biggest headache of them all."

She frowned.

"Oh, don't get all righteous on me. Alcohol is a huge problem up here. You know that by now. And the Natives don't seem to have the genetics to cope with it. Sad, I'm sure, to the bleeding hearts. To cops like me? It's the biggest problem we face. It's a war out there."

Dace didn't agree. Yes, alcohol was a problem. A big one. But it didn't excuse the cops. She'd been reading the stories the *Anchorage Daily News* got a Pulitzer for. Policing in Alaska was as racist as it got. But she wasn't going to argue with crazy. She'd learned that long ago.

"So why the insurance policy then?" she asked. "If you agreed with Campbell why did you think you'd need it?"

He looked out the window. She wasn't sure he was going to answer. Then he turned back to her. "Because I could see that he was going to need a fall guy eventually. The insurance policy was supposed to convince him to look at someone else, not at me."

"And then Luke Kitka?"

"Ah hell, they set that poor bastard up. If you want proof? Look at the blood work. Duke tried to destroy all the copies of that report, but I doubt he got them all. I think the ADA had his own insurance policy."

Jesus, she thought. She didn't swear much, but Jesus help us all.

"So, they," she emphasized "they." "Doped him up and dumped him at the turnout. Then you're sent to shoot him."

"Pretty much, yeah," he said wearily. "They couldn't just murder the tribal president's son without triggering an investigation. Plausible deniability."

He sighed. "Wasn't even the first man I'd killed for Duke. Wasn't the last, for that matter. But it was then I knew there would be a day of reckoning, and that Duke Campbell would let me take the fall for everything. Then I did my research. Developed my insurance policy. Started stashing money. And then Duke found himself a new hatchet man, and he set me up."

"I was wondering about that. Are you sure Duke set you up or did Mike decide he wanted your connection to the boss?"

Petras looked at her. "Huh. Possibly. Doesn't matter. I'm out of it."

Dace called in to the tower in Ketchikan and requested a runway to land. "Go ahead," the friendly voice said, and gave her instructions. "Welcome to Ketchikan International Airport."

Petras chuckled. "One runway and a tower, but damn it's an international airport."

Dace smiled, focused on the landing checklist. "You got a plan for what happens next?"

"I always got a plan," he said.

That was what scared her.

"I could just let you out, take back off again," she offered. "You could just give me the goods now."

He looked at her, smiling. "So now you think I have them. That I didn't mail them ahead?"

She shook her head. "I've been thinking about it," she said. "I think it was all in the bank. Two safety boxes maybe. But you wanted to be able to get to it, in case it all blew up. You've known Campbell was unstable for some time."

Petras sighed. "Yeah, f—king paranoid control freak. And it's been getting worse these last few years. Everyone could see it, but no one wanted to be the one who set off the explosion."

Dace nodded. She bit her lip in concentration as she taxied to a stop. "So just go," she suggested. "Just hand me the package under your jacket and walk away."

He smiled sadly. "I'd like to, girl — no lie. But you know that's not what's going to happen, don't you?"

Dace had been afraid of this. "You going to shoot me sitting here?" she said. "I can open a mic to the tower with a push of the button, and they'll be here in seconds. You won't get away at all then."

His smile broadened. "You're quite the quick thinker," he said. He considered her. "So, what if I give you the papers? What will you do with them?"

Dace shrugged. "What I told you. Fly back, give them to Paul. Let him take down Campbell. He'll be so busy doing that, you'll be able to be on your way," she added.

"True enough." He considered it, holding the gun pointed at her. She sat very still. Then he shrugged. "OK," he said, surprising Dace. Surprised himself maybe, she thought.

He pulled out two packages. Handed her the heftier one. "Good luck with that," he said. "I wish I could be around to watch Duke Campbell go down, but I'd rather be on a beach in Mexico."

He slid out of the plane and onto the ground, and without looking back headed into the terminal. Dace sat still and just breathed for a moment. She had been so sure he would shoot her. Trembling a bit, she looked at the packet on the seat. Maybe it had the goods on Campbell, maybe not. But she wasn't going to wait around to look.

"Air control, I'm headed back to Sitka," she said.

The temptation was great to keep on flying and head home to Talkeetna. But she'd have to fuel in Sitka anyway, and Paul wasn't going to be any happier with her in Talkeetna. Less.

She kept glancing at the manila envelope Hank Petras had left with her. Was there anything in it? Was it just a wad of blank paper? She gritted her teeth and flew into Sitka.

She wasn't surprised someone was waiting for her when she landed. That it was Lanky? Maybe a bit. He and Paul's partner, Joe Bob Dixon, were out at the tie down she taxied back to — less than two hours after she had left it.

She crawled out of the cockpit, and Lanky helped her down. "You OK?" he asked. He hugged her.

She nodded. "Scared out of my wits," she admitted. "But I'll get over it."

She handed the manila envelope to Joe Bob. "Here, you take custody of this."

"What is it?" Joe Bob said, automatically taking the package.

"It's supposed to be all the evidence Hank Petras collected against Duke Campbell," she said shakily. Now that she had Lanky to lean on, it was all beginning to sink in. "I haven't looked. Could be nothing but blank paper."

Joe Bob opened up the envelope and slid out the papers. "Well, they aren't blank," he said with awe. "God damn, I think they're what we've been missing."

He looked at her. "You look like you could use a shower, a change of clothes, and maybe a nap."

"And a sandwich," she said with feeling. They started walking toward the terminal. Dace was afraid Joe Bob would walk into a wall or something if he didn't start looking where he was going instead of at the evidence file.

"And Paul?" she said in a small voice. "Is he mad at me?"

"Why would he be mad at you?" Joe Bob said absently. "Worried sick, I suspect. Captain sent us out here when Jonas came running up to the house. Captain made us get over here. Said to wait here, no matter how long."

Lanky looked at her with sympathy. He probably had a better idea of what scared her. "I was about ready to fire up the other plane and go looking for you," he said. "But tower said you'd filed a flight plan to Ketchikan, and that you didn't appear to be under duress. So, I thought I'd wait a bit. Joe Bob here put in a call to Ketchikan for them to pick up Petras if they could, and to rescue you. They called back and said they missed him, but that you were headed back this way."

Joe Bob nodded. "Been a bit tense around here, no lie."

Dace remembered one piece of news. "I need to see your captain," she said urgently. "There's something else."

Joe Bob looked at his phone. "He's probably pulling up out front. We've had tribal drivers."

Dace was practically running by the time they cleared the airport and out to the sidewalk.

Captain Wyckoff was actually smiling at her. "Good to see you made it back," he said.

She nodded, impatient with the courtesies. "Look, there's something you need to know. The person Petras went to for help after we left the boat? Rosemary. That woman Paul calls Aunt Rosemary? She drove us to the bank and then to the airport."

Wyckoff got very still. "Well, now," he said. "That explains a few things."

"So, do these documents, Captain," Joe Bob added. "I need my computer."

Chapter 25

(Sitka back at the dock. Wednesday.)

Paul Kitka watched helplessly as Hank Petras forced Dace to go with him.

"Damn it," he said. He kept the pressure on Mike Anderson's chest. He was going to bleed out. A few inches different and he'd be dead already.

"Jonas, you've got to go for help. Mom's place is probably as close as any. Call 911, see if she knows where Captain Wyckoff is," he ordered.

Jonas nodded. "On it." He leaped for the dock, cinched the boat up to the cleat, and started up the ramp at a run.

Mike opened his eyes. "Don't let Petras go," he said spitting out the words between gasps for air.

Paul looked at him. "Leave you to die? And do what? He's got a gun, and as he proved with you, he'll use it."

"He's a bad cop."

"Yeah. So are you. Seems like a lot of that going around this town," Paul said sourly.

"Not a bad cop, just doing what needs to be done to clean up the department. Get rid of the bad apples," Mike forced out.

Paul raised his eyebrows. "You do realize that everything Petras has done has been at the direction of Duke Campbell? Right?"

Mike moved restlessly. "No, not true. He's been a loose cannon, and Duke just didn't realize it was him that was causing all this."

Paul snorted. Shook his head. "Right. For 15 years? 20? In this town? People don't even breathe without Duke, Ben Daniels and Swede knowing about it. He was following orders. Just like you are. Duke told you to get rid of Petras. Tells you to do something about me, Jonas. You're his new hatchet man."

"You've got it all wrong," Mike insisted, and then fell silent.

Paul listened carefully. Still breathing. But there was a rattle sound that he didn't like. He needed an ambulance now.

It seemed like forever, but Paul conceded it was probably only 15 minutes. Jonas had moved fast, and the response time was excellent. He'd have to share that with Campbell.

The EMTs started Anderson on some oxygen and took him up the dock on a gurney. When Paul stood up, his hands splattered with blood to go with the filth on the rest of him, he looked up the ramp and there was his captain.

"Welcome back," Wyckoff said quietly. "Come up to the house, we're comparing notes."

"He took Dace," Paul said. "I need to go after her."

"Jonas told me, but Petras moved fast. They flew off the island," Wyckoff said, as they walked up toward the Kitka home.

"What?" Paul said. "He must have had help."

Wyckoff nodded. "Yes. We're not sure who."

"Why would Dace fly him somewhere? I assume that's what you're saying. She knows better than that."

Wyckoff took a few steps in silence. "I was hoping you could tell us that. Are we sure she's still under duress?"

That took a bit for Paul to process. "Are you saying she flew off for other reasons? Like what? Money? In Lanky's plane? She wouldn't trade everything she's built in her life for money."

"OK," Wyckoff seemed to accept Paul's judgment. "Any idea where he might be headed?"

"No," Paul said, still trying to wrap his brain around Dace aiding Petras' escape. She was wilier than that, he thought. She could have escaped. Especially if Petras stopped somewhere to get some help. Why didn't she run?

"Paul," his boss said. "Focus. Where would Petras go?"

"He'd have to stop at his bank for his getaway stash," Paul said.

"Yes."

"So, he has money, and a ride. But Dace can't take him very far in that plane. Ketchikan maybe. He could get a flight out of Ketchikan to anywhere in the world. Well, he can," Paul paused and calculated it out, "at 9 a.m., 2 p.m., or 5:30. What time is it?"

"It's nearly 7 p.m.," Wyckoff answered. "You have the airlines schedule memorized?"

Paul laughed. "An hour later than Sitka and has been the same since they added the third flight when I was a teenager. Why change?"

"So, he probably missed the 5:30 flight," Wyckoff smiled. It was the smile of a hunter who has spotted his prey. "Excellent. He'll have to go to ground in Ketchikan overnight. I've got officers looking for him down there."

Paul didn't say anything, but he wasn't going to count on anyone catching Hank Petras until he got a call that the man was in handcuffs. He did some more calculations, and then looked at his boss. "Wait, if it's that late, Dace should be on her way back. I need to get out to the airport!"

"I already sent Lanky and Joe Bob," Wyckoff said. "How about you take a shower, and then we'll go out. Abbott's here, and he's taken on guard duty for your mom and your sisters."

"Guard duty? Why do they need to be guarded?" Paul demanded as he opened the door to be greeted by his mother a full embrace. He hugged her tightly. How could he have detached himself from this, he wondered. Oh, he could tell himself that he saw them regularly when they came to Anchorage. But the truth was those visits were two-three times a year. It wasn't the same as being an active part of their lives. Of being woven into this place they'd grown up in. His sisters — at some point Deborah must have gotten into town, he noted — piled on him too. He looked at Jonas and laughed. Then he reached out one arm and pulled him into the group hug. Family.

Chapter 26

(Sitka. Airport on Mt. Edgecombe. Wednesday.)

Dace was pleased that the driver Wyckoff had was the same man who had picked Paul and her up at the airport just a few days before. She didn't even know for sure what day it was but felt stupid asking. It was just her and Wyckoff in this car. Lanky and Joe Bob were in the car they'd come in.

"You empty out Talkeetna for this?" Dace asked Wyckoff as she got in the back seat. He took the front. Obviously, he was getting comfortable with how things worked here.

Wyckoff laughed. "Got a couple of Lanky's pilots here, too. They just missed you out at the island, apparently."

"Really? How did they narrow it down?" Dace exclaimed.

"I had a little chat with some flyboys out at the Coast Guard base," Wyckoff said. "They were quite forthcoming. But all that can wait until we get back to the house. Tell everything once. I think you may have brought us the missing pieces of evidence. Well done, Ms. Marshall, well done."

"Not sure that's the reaction I was expecting," Dace said in a small voice.

Wyckoff snorted. "Well, expect Paul to yell at you a bit. He's damn worried. Wanted to come tearing out here after you, but I suggested he needed a shower first. He had blood down the front of him. I left him in a group hug with his family."

Paul in a group hug? Dace thought. Things had changed. He wasn't particularly warm and fuzzy. Girlfriends notwithstanding.

"OK," Dace said, and put her head back and fell asleep.

When Wyckoff woke her as they turned onto Elizabeth's street, Dace wasn't sure the 15-minute nap had done her much good. She needed more than that. Much more.

Wyckoff guided her up the walkway with Lanky and Joe Bob following behind. She tried not to laugh as Joe Bob stumbled because he was looking at Petras' files rather than his feet. She looked at Lanky, who rolled his eyes, but managed to keep the younger man upright.

Inside Elizabeth's house, Dace stayed near the door, trying not to give in to the urge to flee. Who are all these people? she thought in a panic. The room was crowded but no one seemed to mind. She minded!

Then she realized she did know most of them. Rafe, Elijah? What were they doing here? And Bill Abbott?

It was Bill who saw her and grinned. He gave her two thumbs up.

She relaxed a bit. She looked around the room; there were a number of Native Alaskan men who looked like Paul and Jonas. So that's what they'll look like at 50, she thought. Then seeing the old man who had to be Luke Kitka, Sr., tribal president, and Paul's grandfather, she could visualize Paul at 80 as well. She wanted to laugh. The young woman with the baby sitting on the floor at his feet must be Paul's other sister. Dace couldn't remember her name, but the baby was named after Paul.

"Why don't I remember?" Paul was asking his mother. "I've dealt with kids who have been kidnapped. They're traumatized. Terrified."

Lanky Purdue nodded and looked at his son-in-law. Bill Abbott just looked sad. Lanky's daughter had been kidnapped when she was just a little older than Paul had been. She was still terrified if she had to leave Talkeetna or even her house. Going to Anchorage to see Dace fly had been a big deal for her.

Elizabeth Kitka frowned. "I don't know," she said. "I assumed it was because it was someone you knew. That you weren't afraid of. For 30 years, I've looked at everyone, wondering."

Paul shook his head, trying to recall those early days of his life. Hard to remember being four. "The only time I remember being away from home was those days I stayed with Aunt Rosemary," he said in frustration. "Why don't I remember?"

Elizabeth looked at Seth. "She left as soon as I brought out the box."

Seth nodded. He looked sick. "That's how they knew to come looking for something."

"What?" Paul demanded, not following.

"Paul, we never let you stay overnight with Rosemary, most certainly not at four. We rarely went anywhere we didn't take you all with us. You occasionally went out with your grandfather and father hunting or fishing. But even that wasn't at four."

Paul looked at her, struggling to grasp what his mother was trying to tell him.

"What? You're saying Rosemary was my kidnapper?" he demanded. "Rosemary?!"

Elizabeth held Seth's hand tightly. "We used to laugh that the first thing you wanted to do when you were given back was go see Rosemary. I think petting the dog came next."

Stunned, Paul looked at his boss.

Wyckoff turned to Dace. "Rosemary was who Hank Petras went to for help getting to the bank and off the island. He had Dace at gunpoint, and she didn't even blink. Or call us, once she was away from him."

"She a large well-dressed woman?" Joe Bob asked his partner. Paul nodded, still looking stunned.

"Probably the woman with Ben Daniels and Duke Campbell last night," Joe Bob told his boss.

Wyckoff nodded. "Go see the ADA, get a warrant for her arrest. Rosemary Clausen. She owns a shop downtown. Find her. Bring her to the judge's courtroom on Lake Street. I think we're going to need a big space."

"On it," Joe Bob said, his demeanor much quieter than usual as he left the house.

Elizabeth leaned against Seth, her breathing uneven.

"You OK, Mom?" Paul said with alarm. She and Rosemary had been friends for nearly 40 years. Best friends.

"I am f-cking furious," she said, enunciating her words carefully. "She has pretended to be my friend for all these years, and she kidnapped my son!"

Dace said quietly, "A person can be more than one thing. They compartmentalize."

"Mom, I think it's worse than that," Jonas said in the silence.

"Worse? How could it be worse? She kidnapped my son to blackmail my husband!"

"Probably she was only in on the childcare aspect," Paul began.

"Only!"

Jonas tried again. "We've always wondered why Dad was out there with a gun, drunk during morning commute time. Karin found the blood toxicity test. He was doped to the gills."

Elizabeth nodded. She started to say something, but Jonas went on.

"Karin and I speculated that he must have discovered something, who knows what, to indicate who the kidnappers were. He confronted them, and they drugged him. Then dumped him holding a gun with no bullets."

Paul looked sick. Elizabeth looked bewildered.

"You're thinking he confronted Rosemary," Paul said.

Jonas nodded. "And she drugged his drink and then called in her partners."

Elizabeth's face hardened. Her eyes sharpened, and she clenched her fists. "I will kill her," she said calmly. "I will see her dead."

Captain Wyckoff tactfully took no notice of the woman before him who was threatening murder. His phone rang, and he answered.

"Judge," he said respectfully, and then listened. "We'll be there."

"The judge wants us in chambers at 8 p.m.," Wyckoff said. "All of us."

He turned to Luke Kitka, Sr. "He didn't mention you, sir, but I feel if anyone has the right to see justice done today, it is you and the tribal council. Will you join us? Are there others who should be there?"

Luke Kitka, Sr. glanced at two of his relatives, and made a quick flick of his chin. The young men went out the door silently. "They'll find them."

"Then we should go," Elizabeth said. "Getting all of us there will take some time."

People began to file out. Paul spotted Dace and stopped beside her. "I was so afraid for you," he said. "So afraid I would lose you."

Dace reached up and touched his face. "I was afraid you'd be angry with me," she said shakily.

"Angry?" he said incredulously. "Oh, Dace." He pulled her into a tight hug.

"I don't suppose I have time for a shower," she muttered into his shoulder. He had had one. But then, he'd been covered with blood, Captain Wyckoff had said. While she was just filthy and stinky. "And a sandwich?"

"No time for a shower, I'm afraid," Elizabeth said. "But eat this."

Dace took the sandwich gratefully.

Chapter 27

(Sitka. Ben Daniels.)

"Ben, there's a police officer here to see you," his secretary said nervously.

Ben looked up from his desk, and around the office he'd built to suit him. Looked at his secretary. "It will be OK, Mary," he said gently. "Why don't you go home early? I doubt I'll be back today."

She nodded. "If you're sure. Do you want me to call somebody?"

He shook his head. Who would he call? His attorney? He considered that for a moment, and then sighed. He was just so damn tired of this whole mess. Let what happens happen, he thought.

He thought about the beginning. When he was young and ready to make Sitka amount to something. And now? What a mess. Then he reconsidered. Actually? Sitka was doing just fine. And he had played a role in that. But his role was done. Maybe that was OK.

Or maybe he had one last thing to do. With that thought, he checked the weapon he had been carrying and made sure there was a bullet chambered.

Then he straightened his jacket to make sure no bulge showed and walked out into the front office.

"Yes?" he said.

"The judge has requested that you join him in chambers at 8 p.m.," the officer said nervously. "Chief sent me to get you."

Ben looked at the clock. It was 7:45 p.m.

"I think I'll take my own car, if you don't mind," he said. He didn't want to be at the mercy of the Sitka police right now. "I know the way."

"I think, Chief Campbell wanted to see you first," the officer began, and then stopped at the expression on Ben's face. "Yes, sir. I'll tell him."

Ben nodded.

As the officer left the room, Ben called out, "Wait, who else has the judge requested attend this meeting?"

"Just about everybody, sir," he said, and continued out the door.

Ben followed behind him, taking care to lock the door.

In the parking lot, he hesitated and looked at his watch. He had time to walk. The boardwalk along the bay was practically as quick as finding parking would be.

It was a walk he loved. He set out, his stride confident and sure. He'd walked it many times, often into town for a meeting or to have lunch with someone. The bay was to his left. The ships with their boomers and masts silhouetted against the setting sun. The town was directly in front of him.

He loved this town, second only to his kids. Probably more than his wife, he admitted to himself, but he was sure that wouldn't surprise her any. He'd built this town, and he was proud of it. His kids had liked a song in the '80s that always stuck in his brain. He probably wouldn't like the lyrics if he actually knew them all, but he had always liked the lines of the chorus: Starship singing "We Built This City." He hummed it now. He was committed, he realized. He would do whatever was necessary to secure the future of this city, even at the expense of his own dreams of a retirement on warmer beaches.

The bailiff at the front door of the courthouse recognized him and let him in without ID and without checking for weapons. Ben Daniels nodded gratefully. "Don't want to be late for the judge," he said.

"No, sir," the man said. "Especially not tonight. He's on a tirade about having to stay this late."

Ben nodded appreciatively. "Can't say I blame him."

Chapter 28

(Sitka. Wednesday, 8 p.m.)

The Judge was in his robes and sat behind the bench. He looked stern. Joe Bob was standing formally to one side by the bailiff. Rosemary was standing between the two.

"Is this everybody?" the judge asked. "It must be. Looks like most of the town is here." He nodded at the clerk.

"The court is now in order. Judge Robert Cast presiding," the clerk announced.

"This is formally an inquiry into a request for a warrant for the arrest of Rosemary Clausen for the kidnapping of a child. However, my questions will be broader than that. Officer Dixon? Could you please take the stand and summarize your findings for the record?"

Joe Bob had taken the time to go back to the hotel and put on his uniform before approaching the judge. Now he took the stand with his notes in hand.

"Your honor, we have in our possession copies of blood work and other documents pertaining to the death of Luke Kitka, Jr., and to the supposed suicide of two men in jail in the 1980s, as well as to the kidnapping of Paul Kitka as a child.

"All of this cumulated in an attempt to frame Jonas Kitka for the supposed death of Hank Petras, and then to frame Paul Kitka and Candace Marshall for a supposed jail break, and finally the kidnapping and attempted murder of all three of them.

"Luke Kitka, Jr.'s blood toxicity report showed that he had been drugged. This was never presented at the inquest. Nor was the ballistics report that showed the gun found beside him after his death had not been fired."

He looked at the judge. "I'd like to play a tape that was played at the inquest, if I may."

The judge nodded. "Yes, please do. That was before my time."

Joe Bob cued something up on his laptop. "We will, of course, provide you with all of the documentation and chain of evidence," he said. "My understanding is that this is not a formal proceeding at this point, but rather an informational presentation for your consideration."

"So noted."

As Joe Bob Dixon played the dispatch tape of Hank Petras shouting for Kitka to drop the gun, and the shots that quickly fired, Elizabeth Kitka flinched with each shot. Seth Jones, sitting next to her, took her hands. She smiled at him gratefully.

Paul looked grim. Dace had been right, he thought, I should have gone back through the evidence a long time ago and looked at it as a cop, rather than as a teenaged boy. That tape was hard to listen to, in part because it was so damning. Petras had no intention of giving the man time to drop the gun. He'd gone out there on orders to kill.

"We have in our possession a signed statement from Petras stating that he had been ordered to go out that morning and take care of Kitka, permanently," Joe Bob continued.

People in the courtroom erupted into chaos. "Quiet down," the judge ordered. And gradually people silenced.

"Is there any indication as to why such an order was given?" the judge asked.

"Petras wrote that Kitka had been present at a bar the night before and overheard a conversation that revealed the identity of the kidnappers of Paul Kitka, his son, when Paul was four years old. Kitka had gone to confront the kidnapper. She, according to Petras' statement, drugged his drink as they discussed his allegations. She then called Duke Campbell to come and get rid of him."

A lot of murmurs.

"Luke Kitka went to someone's house who he thinks may have kidnapped his son and has a drink with her?" The judge sounded incredulous.

"The alleged kidnapper was a close friend of the family," Joe Bob explained. "I believe he would have been unable to believe she was involved, and more than willing to listen to any explanation she might offer. He had already been drinking that evening, which would further reduce his critical thinking abilities."

"All right. So, what was the motive for the kidnapping?" The judge asked. "Do we know?"

"That goes back to the early 1980s. During a meeting between the Borough Assembly, Tlingit tribal elders, and the chief of police, a fight broke out. Dozens were arrested, others were injured, including two officers. When the assistant district attorney reviewed the arrests, he ordered them released, and announced an investigation into police brutality. Ostensibly, two men were found dead, declared suicides, and disposed of. Those men were never properly identified, there were no autopsies, and the bodies were never released to their families. One of the men was a police chief from White Swan, Washington. Luke Kitka was prepared to testify about them, their presence in the jail, and their disappearance. He was blackmailed into silence by the kidnapping."

Joe Bob looked at the judge. "This is an informal summarization of the documents we have in our possession," he repeated his earlier stipulation. "All of the materials will be turned over to the district attorney's office in Juneau for review so that formal charges may be brought."

"Noted. What are you asking for today?"

"We would like arrest warrants issued to take people into custody whom we believe might be flight risks," he replied.

The back door of the courtroom opened, and three uniformed state patrol officers entered. "And you are?" the judge asked.

"Sorry to be late, Judge Case," the lieutenant in charge said. "We are here to assist Captain Wyckoff in his investigation into the kidnapping of Officer Paul Kitka, Fish and Game Warden Jonas Kitka, and Candace Marshall. I've been at the hospital waiting to see if assistant police chief Mike Anderson would survive the gunshot he took to the chest today. The doctors believe he will. He is, however, heavily sedated and was unable to answer any questions."

"And do we have a suspect in that shooting?" the judge asked, a bit of sarcasm.

"A warrant has gone out to the Ketchikan police for the arrest of Sitka Police Officer Hank Petras for attempted murder."

"This would be the Petras that was supposedly killed by Jonas Kitka last week," the judge said, his sarcasm deepening.

"Yes, sir." The Juneau lieutenant's reply was equally dry.

"All right." The judge looked at the assistant district attorney. "Let's drop those charges against Jonas Kitka. It's embarrassing to have warrants out for the arrest of one man for killing a man we have warrants out for attempting to kill another man."

The ADA nodded.

The judge turned back to Joe Bob. "So, what you're telling me is that 30 plus years ago two men died in the Sitka jail, under suspicious circumstances, and that the investigation was derailed by the kidnapping of a key witness's young son. Then 15? 20? years ago, that witness discovers who the kidnappers were, and is killed by a police officer in a staged situation."

"Yes, sir."

"And this all comes back to a head this week, why?"

"We believe that Jonas Kitka and Karin Wallace, the daughter of the White Swan police chief, may have triggered it by requesting all the materials around both deaths from the district attorney's office. The co-conspirators may have been afraid of what would be discovered in these records." Joe Bob spread his hands out and added, "That is speculation, of course. Their panic may have escalated with the arrival of State Patrol Lieutenant Paul Kitka."

"So, then they kidnap them and dump them in Tongass, as a way of containing the situation?" The judge was incredulous. "Did they think the disappearance of a state patrol lieutenant would go unquestioned?"

Joe Bob shrugged. "We would like to ask them that as well."

"Fine," the judge said. "I believe there is enough evidence for the arrests of the parties involved, pending formal charges by the DA's office." He looked at the ADA stationed in Sitka. "Will you be handling that?"

The ADA shook his head. "No sir. I'm sure I'll be called to assist, but the DA himself will be lead on this investigation."

Judge Case looked at Duke Campbell, standing in the back surrounded by four officers in their dark uniforms and tactical wear. He frowned. Then he looked at Captain Wyckoff.

"Captain Wyckoff? Will you list the names of those you're seeking arrest warrants for?"

"Yes, sir," Wyckoff said, coming to the table in front. The ADA looked up at Wyckoff. "Do you want to enlighten me?" he said dryly.

Wyckoff looked at him silently. "I'd like to have warrants for the murder of Luke Kitka, Jr., Andrew Solomon, and Jacob Wallace. In addition to the kidnapping of the child Paul Kitka."

"And who will you be serving the warrants on?" the judge's voice was dry.

"Ben Daniels, Rosemary Clausen, and," he hesitated and took a deep breath, "Police Chief Duke Campbell."

"Additional warrants will be needed for the kidnapping and attempted murder of Candace Marshall, Jonas Kitka, and Paul Kitka," he added. He began to list the conspirators.

The police at the back were the only ones who moved. Shocked, Dace thought. But then they were the only ones who didn't know that was coming. She was watching them, not the judge, so she was the only who saw Duke Campbell pull a gun.

"*Gun!*" she yelled. The young men of the tribe — she had not realized Paul had so many cousins and uncles — moved to protect the tribal elders. No one else moved.

Campbell held the gun steady, pointed at Paul Kitka. Paul just looked at him, keeping his hands away from his body so that no one could claim he was reaching for a weapon of his own. One false move, and Duke's officers would go for their weapons and turn the courtroom into a bloodbath.

No one said anything for a moment.

Then Ben Daniels sighed. "Duke, put the gun down. Shooting him or anyone else isn't going to do you a bit of good. It's over."

"Maybe for you it is," Duke said. "But I'm not going to prison."

Suicide by cop? Paul wondered. Is that what he's looking for? Joe Bob had his weapon out and trained on the chief, although he didn't think Duke saw him. Duke saw Paul. Or, perhaps, he saw Paul's father.

"No, no, prison wouldn't be a good place for a police chief," the bar owner said softly. "You've had a good run, Duke. Nearly 40 years. Not many police chiefs can say that."

"Damn right," Duke said. "What I've done I've done for the best, for Sitka."

"But people aren't going to see it that way," Daniels continued softly. "They are going to judge you now, and not understand the way it was back then. If you go to trial, it will make national headlines. Everyone will judge you. Condemn you. Even ridicule you. Your name will become a joke."

Paul tried not to let his frown escape to his face. Where was Daniels going with this? He didn't like the feel of it.

"I am not a joke." Duke said through clenched teeth. "I made this town. You and I and Swede, we made Sitka flourish. That's what they should remember. Not the death of some town drunk."

"I know, Duke," Daniels continued in that soft persuasive voice. "But you know, and I know, that isn't what will happen. You'll be remembered as a racist and a fool. *If* it goes to trial."

Duke Campbell looked confused for a moment, and then his jaw firmed. Paul tensed. The chief had made up his mind — but to do what Paul wasn't exactly sure.

"No trial," he said clearly, and then he jerked his gun to his mouth, angled it so that the bullet would go through the back his mouth and up through his brain, and pulled the trigger.

As pandemonium broke out, Paul met Daniels' eyes in what felt like an oasis of calmness. Daniels nodded his head once, confirming the unspoken accusation in Paul's eyes. Yes, he'd intentionally talked the unstable man over the cliff. Yes, he had known how Duke would react to his words.

Paul sighed. It would all be put on Duke. Maybe that was OK.

He turned, looking for Dace. Lanky was hustling her out the back door, with commands to his pilots. Bill Abbott? What was he doing here? he thought, wondering why he'd chosen to come along. Wyckoff had said it was Abbott who had been his mother's guard through all this. He didn't like thinking that his mother had needed a guard, but if she did? Bill was a fine one. In fact, even now Bill didn't leave his post by his mother's side.

"Come on boys, Candace," he heard Lanky say. "Let's get on out of here and head back before someone finds a reason to make us stay. We've a got a business to run."

Dace looked back at Paul helplessly, but moved along with her fellow pilots. She could see it was going to be awhile before he got free. If he ever did. She wondered if he realized the judge was looking at him like he might be the answer to his prayers. He would make a fine interim police chief, she acknowledged. Maybe even a permanent one. And that would be poetic justice — a Kitka as chief of police? More than poetic, true justice, indeed.

Where would that leave them? Would he even have time for her in the near future? The recent development between them was so tenuous, so new, it wouldn't survive distance, much less a crazy job where he worked around the clock to restore justice and trust in his home town. And, she acknowledged, she was no Elizabeth Kitka either. Paul's mother had been the strong backbone of the family. One her troubled husband had leaned on. One who saw her children had a good life in spite of the treatment she received from the community and from her husband's family. And she'd done it practically single-handedly. Dace knew herself better. She had too many barely healed wounds to be that kind of strength for her husband and her family. She admired Elizabeth. She wished she could be that strong. But she wasn't.

Talkeetna suited her. It had welcomed her. She had a job, a place to belong. And, yes, perhaps there, she and Paul would have a chance to explore a future together.

But not here. She wasn't strong enough for Sitka.

Paul looked around the room. Joe Bob and Wyckoff were talking the police officers out of their weapons. He moved in that direction, then realized he was a bit shaky. Having a gun pointed at you would do that. And it wasn't even the first gun he'd had pointed his direction today. He'd just stand here and let his boss and partner take care of the officers. Wouldn't that be a clean-up job! There wasn't an officer among them worth keeping on. Paul shuddered, not envying the man who got stuck with that.

His sisters were sitting with their mother, who was pale but completely reserved, ignoring her supposedly best friend who was kneeling beside her, pleading for understanding. Paul thought Rosemary had better move away before Angela decked her.

"You don't know what it was like to be a single woman in this town," she said. "I had no choice but to go along with whatever they said. What else could I do? They brought Paul to me, and I figured he was safer with me than with them! Elizabeth? Please, listen to me."

Elizabeth looked at her for a long moment. "You kidnapped my son, blackmailed my husband, and then you had him killed, leaving me with four children to finish raising alone, without their father," she said levelly. "But it's all about you. It always was, wasn't it? How did I never see that?"

She looked up at Bill Abbott, who was standing nearby. "Get her away from me," she said.

"Yes, ma'am," he said. Bill bent over, lifted Rosemary to her feet, and then handed her over to the bailiff. "You should arrest her," he advised.

"Not my job," the man stammered. Wyckoff gestured to Joe Bob who read the woman her rights.

The judge looked over to the tribal elders. "Justice will be done," he told them. "I'm very sorry it has taken this long."

"Paul, you need to go after her," Jonas's voice said over his shoulder.

Paul looked back at him, still shocked by the rapid events. "After who?"

"Dace," Jonas said impatiently. "Don't just stand there like a dufus. Go after her."

Paul hesitated. Things had been easier when they were in the middle of nowhere. Betrayal didn't seem possible then. Now? He looked at his mother, who was stone-faced as the woman she'd called friend sobbed and pleaded with her to understand. How could you ever really know who to trust?

"You can't," Jonas said matter-of-factly, and Paul realized he must have said the last out loud. "That's why they call it trust. You have to risk it. And if you're not in the co-pilot's seat when she lifts off, in oh, about 30 minutes, you're going to kick yourself for the rest of your life."

Jonas looked around the room. "For one thing, someone is going get the bright idea that you'd make a fine interim police chief to clean up this mess."

Appalled, Paul looked at his brother. "I'm not doing that," he protested, keeping his voice down. "It would take months! Years, even."

Jonas tossed him car keys. "Then go," he ordered. "I'll get the car later."

Paul snatched the keys, hesitated a bit more, looking at his mother. "Take care of Mom, won't you? This will hit her hard."

One of the Juneau troopers had Rosemary in custody, but she was fighting him, wanting to continue talking to Elizabeth. Paul hesitated.

"Paul! Go, God damn it!"

And Paul went. "Bill?" he called over his shoulder. "You want a ride?"

Dace was running down her checklist for takeoff, when the co-pilot door opened. Paul hopped in.

"Hi," he said.

She tilted her head and a slow smile started. "Hi."

"Let's go home," he said.

Postscript

Hi, I'm the author of this book, and I hope you liked it. I lived in Alaska as a newspaper reporter and fell in love with the state and its people. Sitka is one of the most beautiful places in the world — even if you do need a boat or plane to get more than 15 miles from home.

If you liked the book, please write a review for wherever you bought this book. Or put in a good word for the book on your Facebook page or social media site. Epublishing works because people sing out when they find books they like.

And stay in touch: you can subscribe to my Telling Stories newsletter[1] — there's a free short story as a signing bonus — or by visiting me at www.ljbreedlove.com[2] where you'll find my other books, a blog, and free stuff!

Paul and Candace will be back, but in the meantime, there are other stories you can check out on my website.

Thanks again for reading this book.

L.J. Breedlove

---

1.   https://ljbreedlove.com/pages/index.php/newsletter-subscription/

2.   http://www.ljbreedlove.com/

Also by L.J. Breedlove

Interludes
When Ryan Met Master A
Kaleidoscope of Memory
Baby Ruby
Fire Drill

Newsroom PDX
Choose
Don't Go
Hold Me
Rage
Be the Change
In Charge
When Ryan Met Ruby

Newsroom PDX Omnibus
PDX 2020 Fall
PDX 2021 Winter
PDX 2021 Spring
Truth to Power

PDX Year 2
Do the Job
Hear Me
Miss You
Memory
Hunted
Seen

Past Lives
Life in Focus

PDX Year 3
Smart Girl
Hero
A Story Well Told
Who Do I Tell?
My Body
A Literary Life
Will Anyone Hear?

Talkeetna
Everybody Lies
Somebody's Secrets
Nobody Cares
Nobody's Fool
Is Anybody Alive?
Dead Tourist
Talkeetna

Wolf Harbor
Woman of Hat Island
Alpha Female
Alpha's Alpha
Power Grab
Safe Haven
Missing Pieces

Beta Wolf
Girls School
I Love You Two

Wolf Harbor Rescue
Seek and You Shall Find
To Have and to Hold
All the Hidden Places

About the Author

L.J. Breedlove is a former journalist writing mysteries and thrillers about what she knows: complicated people, small towns, big cities, cops, reporters, politicians, assorted bad guys.

"I write about religion and politics. About race and gender. I believe in the journalism axiom: Comfort the afflicted, and afflict the comfortable. To which the labor organizer Mother Jones was supposed to have added: And in general raise hell. That works for me."

L.J. grew up on a cattle ranch and then went to college to be an oceanographer. She decided getting seasick was not a good trait for an oceanographer to have, and discovered journalism instead — a field that liked people who asked questions!

As a reporter and editor, she worked in Alaska, Oregon, Idaho, Texas, Washington, D. C. Then she got homesick for the Pacific Northwest and came home to work with college newspapers and teach journalism.

She is an over-educated, bleeding heart liberal with a penchant for heroes such as Jack Reacher. She isn't particularly bothered by the inconsistency.

You can follow her on Twitter @ljbreedlove for her political stuff, or on Facebook ljbreedlove for her writing life. Best place to find her -- besides a local coffee shop -- is at ljbreedlove.com. You can sign up for her email newsletter there. Or read her blog, snark included, and check out all her books.

Made in the USA
Columbia, SC
02 January 2024

29775766R00140